The Geometer
Lobachevsky

To Susan

ALSO BY ADRIAN DUNCAN

Midfield Dynamo
A Sabbatical in Leipzig
Love Notes from a German Building Site

The Geometer Lobachevsky

ADRIAN DUNCAN

TUSKAR ROCK PRESS

First published in Great Britain in 2022 by
Tuskar Rock Press,
an imprint of Profile Books Ltd
29 Cloth Fair
London
ECIA 7JQ
www.serpentstail.com

First published in Ireland by The Lilliput Press

Note on the text: This is a work of fiction. All characters, businesses, organisations, artworks and events portrayed in this novel are either products of the author's imagination or are used fictitiously.

Set in 12.5 pt on 17.5 pt Fournier by iota (www.iota-books.ie)

10 9 8 7 6 5 4 3 2 1

Printed and bound in Great Britain by Clays Ltd, Elcograf S.p.A.

The moral right of the author has been asserted.

A CIP catalogue record for this book is available from the British Library.

ISBN 978 1 78816 972 1
eISBN 978 1 78283 942 2

FSC
www.fsc.org
MIX
Paper from
responsible sources
FSC® C018072

'It's been such a long time since we met,' the bishop observed, tenderly stroking his mother's arm and shoulder. *'When I was abroad I missed you, Mother, I really missed you!'*

— 'The Bishop,' Anton Chekhov

A dying man lies prone on a coverless bed in a single-windowed room in the upper floor of a building not far from the sea. The window has been left an inch or two ajar. A rhombus of white moonlight illuminates a portion of wall above the bed, and from the ceiling of this room a glinting mobile of small steel shapes – a circle, a square, a triangle, a pyramid – dangles, clinking gently in the sea air.

In his mind's eye appears the image of a photograph he lost many years before. In the foreground stand five men on the edge of acres of unworked bog. In among these men, all leaning on their implements, stands this man as a younger person. He is smiling, and the wind in the photograph has lifted his dark hair off his forehead into lazy floating strands around his crown.

It is towards these men, over their shoulders and into this broad province of brown earth that the mechanized mind's eye of the dying man proceeds.

PART I

Point of square touches face of pyramid, while in the background a triangle spins past.

1

I am standing on the edge of a bog. There is wind. And sky meeting arm-opening land. Three men stalk out into this dark terrain. One carries a clinking tripod under his arm and two leather cases in his right hand. Another, head down, bears two bundles of timber stakes on his shoulders, as does the other. I hold a sledgehammer and coiled around my left hand are twenty-two yards of steel chain. My shoes, foot-clothes and feet are wet. I trudged with these men through mud of this kind yesterday and the day before and the day before, laying out across this land a giant if invisible triangle.

A gust of wind breaks and rushes at my face. The two men carrying the timbers topple.

The gust passes.

The two men right themselves and gather up their stakes.

One of the points on this triangle has been carved onto an obelisk three yards to the north of a concrete chimney that protrudes from the horizon in the distance – towards the west-south-west, they tell me. It is a huge if slim flue for a power station being built by Germans and on the face of this squat stone obelisk has been inscribed the foot of a crow, with three talons extending down from a horizontal line, the centre of which lies thirty-four feet, six and five-eighths inches above sea level. The second point on this triangle has been carved onto the side of a bridge three miles east of where I stand now. This structure is old and of British construction and they refer to it as Kjaknu Bridge. It carries a railway that runs west to a large town called Galway, and east to the capital city of Dublin, and beneath this cut-stone bridge runs a canal that leads north to a lake and south to another. They tell me this canal once carried boatloads of flax, then boatloads of people, until it fell out of use. Onto the keystone to the northern face of this bridge is carved another crow's foot, at twenty-two feet, eight and one-quarter inches above sea level. These three men and I are struggling to place accurately the third point of our triangle into the middle of this stretch of bog before me.

It has begun to rain. The dark undulating hills in the distance have become shrouded in a mist that opens then rolls around these unimpressive summits. The sky is grey in that drab way I would often see, when I was young, in the sky over the shivering countryside outside my hometown, Kazan, on any morning in early spring. The cheerful clipped voices of these three men disappear skyward as they walk a path trampled between long oily openings in the bog. The land reaches out into further plains of brown and black, and tufts of deep green punctured through with tiny wavering dots of white.

The third man, Kolim, a dark and blue-eyed person, drops a dozen stakes. They make a hollow clatter that seems to trigger from behind me the call of a distant crow or raven or an indigenous bird of some kind whose name I have not yet learned. The second man, Mehl, a balding and bearded person, tips from his arms his stakes, then rubs his hands together while smiling impishly – raising his eyebrows as his thinning dark hair lifts from his forehead and stands for a few shuddering moments, then falls. The first of these country men, Rhatigan, creaks out the legs of his tripod. He speaks calmly to his men as he scans the leaning land, while beckoning me, in turn, out onto it.

When I was sent by the Soviet state to London to further my studies in calculus, knowing I would never become a great mathematician, I strayed instead into the foothills of anthropology. What I lack in my ability now to read numbers I make up for with my ability to read people; and I know these people here will never triangulate this land accurately because this land, as far as I can tell, sits upon a lake, of which they seem completely unaware. When I watch them walking across the surfaces of this place, these people suddenly list or stumble, or some days they simply fall over, as if, unbeknown to them, they are on the deck of an enormous ship heaving upon a distant subterranean ocean on a gusty day. Then they pick themselves up like nothing has occurred and continue on their way. I can feel these small shifts in the ground beneath my feet too on days when the dark seas far below must be rough. I picture descending labyrinths in the hull of this ship, shaking around terrifyingly, scaring the crew hands within. Sometimes, on these choppy days, when Rhatigan invites me to the tripod and I lift my spectacles and look through the lens of the level perched on top, with its crosshairs trained, say, on the centre of a distant chimney pot piercing the ridge of a small thatched house, issuing climbing strings of smoke from its cup, he utters: 'Can you not see that, Nikolai? The chimney, moving across the vertical, then above and below the horizontal.'

'I can,' I usually reply.

'Ground vapour?' he usually asks.

And he always looks doubtful when I nod to his increasingly convenient postulations, and in his doubt he has begun, I feel, molecule by molecule, to see through me. He will soon see that what is in me, is not what I know about the solution here, but what it is I am keeping from him about this problem – that it is the bogland under their feet that is moving and not the buildings in the distance. I will tell him soon that he is better to use the navigation tools of the sea-going vessel here – the sextant, the chronometer. I will tell him, just before I board my train to Dublin on my route back to the Soviet embassy in London, that he is better to turn away from the Euclidean rigidity he has been employing here up to now, because planes of that kind rest too brittlely on soaked-out places such as this.

I pull my collar up on my neck, tug my cap over my spectacles and step down onto the bog.

Rhatigan dangles an inverted bronze cone from the end of a follicle of shining copper. He is in his late forties, grey-haired but well preserved, and entirely engrossed in his work. The plumb, swinging between the legs of the tripod, is seeking in the wind its centre over a ten-foot iron stake that was hammered into the ground the day I arrived. Six inches above the peat hovers a circular head plate with lurid red and white concentric diameters printed upon it. The circumferences decrease to a circle the size of a kopek and in the middle of this circle a tiny dot has been etched, and somewhere within that tiny dot oscillates the secondary benchmark we are trying, in theory, to place into this expanse.

'Look,' says Rhatigan, nodding towards a black cloud rumbling up over the ridge of the distant hill.

'Kolim, Mehl; leave the stakes. We'll take shelter!'

The rain drums onto the roof of Rhatigan's auto as we slough off our coats. The land outside has now disappeared behind this odourless curtain of passing rain. There have been many far more intense storms here this week.

'I had a thought,' says Rhatigan, as Kolim, turning from the front seat, flares a match then lights a cigarette, 'we'll stake out across this parcel in triangles. The parallelograms feel like points too many.'

Kolim exhales a cloud of smoke across the land map upon which Rhatigan has neatly drawn a grid of squares expanding across a segment of near-featureless land. As the smoke lifts, this grid of squares reappears, pinching to a point in the middle of the indicated trunk road – from where stems the corner of another square, leading to others spreading outward across the land and penetrating this bog in which we shelter from the rain. Rhatigan pencils diagonals through an interlinking line of squares; then, he hopscotches his pencil tip across the drawing, ending at a pillar – the entrance to a house burnt down fifteen years before, or so they told me one day, with barely concealed ardour, almost as if they had done it themselves. A 'planters' estate' they called it.

The rain passes and brings with it a weight of air. We pull on our wax jackets and step down again into the glistening bog.

Two hours have passed and the sun is shining. Our coats lie in a mound to the left of Rhatigan who is stooping, in the distance, to the tripod. We have set out fifteen equilateral triangles across this parcel of land and Mehl and Kolim now trudge back to the auto to collect further armfuls of stakes.

It was fifteen years ago when I first met Rhatigan. He was on a state research trip to Kirov, visiting the largest of Glav Torf's peat-extraction works and power stations. He came with another Irish engineer, referred to as Oleeri, and their chief, a large man called Glenin. They had flown in some days earlier from Berlin and had been brought on a tour of institutions in Moscow, then Leningrad, then east to us. I was the de facto receiving dignitary at Kirov. The vice-minister for peat had fallen ill and I was dispatched to take his place. I was then instructed to stay there – one of many confusing and paranoiac demotions during that decade. In Moscow they met Minister Malenkov, then a senior state official, a brute, for whom a few years later I would work briefly at the Special Committee on Rocket Technology. At Kirov, we received message ahead that none of these visiting Irish men drank alcohol, but that luckily they all smoked. We wondered what strangers from distant lands might say to each other over the course of an evening if they cannot drink together. This Rhatigan was with us to learn how to 'win the peat', as he said often.

Each day he'd wake at four, call us from our rooms and would not relent until after ten in the evening. Each night, as if marking the day's progress, he'd drink, with a militant moderation, a glass of milk in our company, before retiring to bed. On his first evening, as if trying to impress on us the special difficulties he faced back in his homeland, he pointed to his glass of milk and claimed that 'there is more dry matter in that glass than in most of the bogs we are aiming to win'. The men from each department at Kirov were glad to see him go. They found his innocent diligence irritating. I accompanied him each day around the land, drainage-systems, railways and works, translating our ideas, processes and problems into English, for him to nod to and make endless notes. I'd observe him as he wrote his lengthy jottings, his head and abdomen bowed into a hunch over his raised thigh, scribbling with a stub pencil into his yellow notebook. On his final night in Kirov, he and I stayed up late, after all of the other delegates had retired to bed. Rhatigan told me about his homeland, the ties they hoped to forge with us, his pride in his new country and the sacrifices they had made. He then told me that he had killed his brother during the Civil War. He and two of his comrades walked this brother, Charles, to the side of a bog and put a bullet into the back of his head. Rhatigan's hands trembled on his lap as he relayed this to me. And as he stood and clumsily made to embrace me, before he left silently for bed, I realized that he had not spoken of this to anyone for some time, if ever. He and his two research colleagues, this Oleeri and this Glenin, left the next morning before I could speak to him again or bid him farewell.

Then, one day some years later, while I was returned to Leningrad once more – this time to revise and re-translate into English a paper my great-grandfather had composed over three-quarters of a century before, on the geometry of curves – I decided to write to this Gunter Rhatigan. I wanted to know how well he had learned from us. I wanted to know how their research trip had served them. I wanted, in truth, to make contact with him again because I had then lost the second of my two only friends – Matvei, a scriptwriter. His passing had compounded the loss of my other friend from years before – Gusev, a sculptor of abstract forms, who had perished in a camp in the north. Some weeks after I sent my letter, Rhatigan responded, informing me that he and his Irish colleagues were doing well, that they had 'drained and won over a large bog in Offaly, and a smaller one of fifteen hectares near Kildare', and that their work, railways, machines and housing projects were on schedule and that they hoped to extend 'into the Midlands', where they intended to continue enacting what they had learned from us in Kirov years before. I wrote back immediately; and this began our years-long correspondence, which has culminated in Rhatigan's recent request for my help in measuring this troublesome piece of land.

Rhatigan approaches flinging his cigarette stub into a puddle.

'Nikolai,' he says, in his thin voice, 'you know you're not obliged to accompany us here all day; we can easily report to you in the office.'

I tell him that I can really only advise on the processes of measurement I see.

'And what would you advise, Nikolai?' he asks. 'Dublin's getting impatient.'

He is smiling a pained smile, the large gap between his front two teeth showing.

'Can you make available an hour in my hotel bar this evening?' I ask, to which he nods.

Kolim and Mehl return and drop their armfuls of stakes at our feet. I pick up the twenty-two yards of chain and we string it out into the wet land. Rhatigan returns to his tripod, steps in behind, pulls focus and indicates Kolim left, then right, then left once more, all the while his head obscured behind the glinting theodolite eye. I wonder, from there, can he see dejection in our expressions. He gestures Kolim to stop with the upraised palm of his hand. It shines white in the sun. Then he points his index finger downward and Kolim pushes a stake into the ground; Mehl thumps it with the sledgehammer, and again. We pin one end of the chain to the stake and walk at an angle out twenty-two yards, until it pulls taut, then we look back to Rhatigan in the mid-distance, still leaning into the tripod, his hand in the air shuffling Kolim over and back in tiny steps around a point somewhere in the black peat below.

2

The front bar of the hotel I'm lodging in for the duration of my visit is quietly hosting the last few billion rays of the day's sun. It is a summer's evening, even though during the day it felt to me like an afternoon from early spring and a morning from late autumn. Groupings of men stand in the light at the end of the bar, smoking cigarettes. More sit to the rear on timber stools eating sandwiches and moment to moment taking sips from glasses of a shining black drink they call 'porter'. Then these small men utter words that are largely indistinct to me. They are affable, but none over the whole of my four weeks here have sat with me. They bid me 'hello' and 'good evening'. The wealthy farmers who come each week from the livestock mart in the town to the east have yet to arrive. Mister Leevee, the owner of this hotel, stands at the bar rubbing down a tap. He is one of the roundest creatures I have ever seen. He moves, if he moves at all, at the rate of schisms. Then, he materializes.

In my leather satchel beside me are bundled my drawing tools: a variety of ropes and ribbons – white, blue, green and red. I have a spool of thread too and a ball of pink wool.

On the table lies open a letter, delivered today, ordering me back to Leningrad to take up a 'special appointment'. The letter is unsigned, merely a stamp on its bottom corner. I finger it a moment and wonder what is being said about me back at the State Geometers' Office and what is being said from those there to those in the MGB offices from where this letter came. In the pit of my stomach bubbles a pool of bile; I want to take a match to this pool, light it and burn it away, then take the match to what remains.

An old gentleman, carrying a hammer and a trophy made of what looks like brass and marble, stomps in through the swinging door of the hotel bar. He is stout and his hindquarters protrude in a way that thrusts the top half of his body forward, as if he smells the world first before he sees it. He approaches the bar and orders a drink, climbs onto a high stool and swings himself out to the floor of the bar, which is simple, dusty, dry. The expansive fireplace at the other end of this irregularly shaped room has, from the broad sticks in its hearth, begun to smoke and crackle. This gentleman, whom I would estimate is in his late sixties, doffs his cloth cap. I am sure I have not seen him before. I nod and return to my notebook. Then I hear his hammer being lifted with a scrape from the bar, and out of instinct I look up.

'I've another thirty of these,' he says, looking at me, waving this small lump hammer beside his large round head.

He thuds the hammer back onto the bar, then fixes his glasses and peers at my notebook as if it were an exotic bird. I push it closed, folding my letter within, and he continues, 'I've thirty of them above in the museum.'

'Hammers,' I reply.

'Thirty, all the same, but different, and those are just for beating lead. I've another thirty for cobbling and building.'

'And the trophy?'

'You're not from the Midlands, are you?'

'I'm visiting from Leningrad – to help Mister Rhatigan … The trophy?' I say.

'Bill Makonel's man-of-the-match award for the '35 county final,' he says. Then he leans forward with a creak, and as his face breaches the shaft of softening sunlight between us, he says, 'Tell me now, boyo: How's Uncle Joe? Still slaughtering away over there, is he?'

I smile.

He sits back.

'I don't like Commies,' he says.

'I don't think of myself as one,' I say.

My friend takes a drink from the porter Mister Leevee had moments earlier placed down on the bar. His little finger is raised as he tips his head back. He swallows, in mechanisms, then pushes the back of his hand across his mouth. Other than Leevee receiving an order from the opposite side of the bar, there is little being said. A horse and cart pulls in off the road. A cluster of children pass, talking quickly as they skip and lurch, one with two upturned metal buckets tied to her bare feet, raising her above the others as if she were on stilts.

'And how's Bermuda treating you out there?'

I look up and see he is smiling at Leevee, who has reappeared at our end of the bar once more. My friend looks back to me, over the rims of his glasses. His eyes are dark and one has been damaged. He looks jaundiced, and I discern he might be a bachelor.

'It's a difficult project,' I reply.

'If it has the beating of Rhatigan, then it must be.'

And there is a pause.

He rubs his lips again, and sips from his glass. He places the porter back, but he is still looking at me, his arm making an awkward shape as he searches for the surface of the bar.

'You know I've Russian bullets from the last war too,' he says.

'In this museum?' I reply. 'I like to visit museums.'

'I don't tell many about it. But then I don't have you down as a thief. Tell Rhatigan to drop you over some evening and I'll give you the grand tour.'

The door swings open to my right again; a tall and slim man enters.

'Shaihmeen, you're early,' he says.

My friend turns, looks over his glasses at the tall and slim man entering and replies, gesturing lazily towards me, 'I'd an urgent meeting with the Russki here.'

'Rhatigan's aide,' says the man, looking down at me.

They greet each other in the way men, I notice, usually greet here – on the cusp of shaking hands until the moment or moments for handshaking ebbs and their bodies relax into a shape that most allows for the sort of idle chatter that seems, between the silences, to flood the place.

I remove my spectacles, rub my eyes, then order another whiskey from Leevee and a glass of porter too. As he turns to prepare my beverages, I grasp my notebook, stand and leave the bar. I go to the front wall of the hotel to take some air. It is warmer outside. There is an old man leaning back on the windowsill, his face turned to the evening sun. He's smoking a cigarette and appears to be in a trance. I bid him a greeting and open out my letter.

'Special appointment,' it says. 'Return to Leningrad and present by the 12th of May inst.'

I try to pinpoint what's finally ruptured the film of seeming untouchability that has protected me since graduation from university. Perhaps they have located my letters to Gusev. We met at army training camp in '37 where we both then also befriended Matvei, the young scriptwriter, frustrated at this year of training keeping him from the work he loved. It was this feeling of fear and frustration that drew the three of us so close. Then, one day Gusev heard his father had been disposed of and the next he himself was gone. It was not until one December morning in '39 that I heard from him again. I had returned home from London and I met my dear Matvei near a train station in Leningrad; he had a stack of unopened letters from Gusev. I wrote back to him immediately, but each letter took a fortnight to arrive at the wood combine, at the farthest reaches of the north, into which poor Gusev had been cast two years before – branded an 'Article 58' subversive. That he was not killed, he claimed in his first letter to me, was 'the greatest miracle of the '30s'. We continued to write for six years, up to his final disappearance, no matter where I was stationed, even during the War when I was hospitalized for months with a snapped shin, then sent to the power station in Kirov once more, to organize the storage of paintings and furniture moved east from the Hermitage. These paintings came without their frames and, as I stacked and itemized each canvas in the cellar in Kirov, I often pictured a multitude of empty frames covering the many walls of the vast Hermitage many hundreds of miles west of the huge and dust-dry cellar where I spent my days. Each of my letters to Gusev was directed through Matvei's uncle, a voluntary at the same wood combine where Gusev was imprisoned. Perhaps, even though Matvei is dead six years, someone has finally unearthed my letters to Gusev.

I fold the official missive away. The old man, who seems to have lifted clear of his trance is now waving to a person approaching on a ticking bicycle. I squint for a few moments at this smudge of dark blue emerging from horizontal bands of grey and brown and green and sky blue. It begins to gather into the shape of a police officer. He pedals into clarity, and dismounts.

'Paskal,' he says.

'Sergeant,' the old man mutters, as he steps past me, returning indoors.

'I didn't see Rhatigan yet today,' says this policeman, a man they call Makaihb. 'He's gone off radar. I needed to call out myself. Can you sign and I'll be on my way.'

As I scribble my name onto this page, he asks, 'And how's the work progressing for ye out yonder?' Then he pulls his watch from his pocket and checks it.

'Very well,' I reply.

'Good men. I'll be off.' And he turns, lifts his bicycle away from the wall and as he pedals across the forecourt and onto the road his form re-disintegrates into a vertical daub of dark blue. It shivers for a while until it swerves then disappears again into the soft broad bands of green and brown and mauve. I return indoors to my table and, as I put my spectacles on, the world around me sharpens back into itself and I can hear the two men at the bar cackle hard.

A few hours later, and I see the bob of a white circle of light belonging to a carbide lamp break the navy darkness outside. The light is suddenly extinguished. The bar is now smoke-filled and raucous. Four of the wealthy farmers who are driving back towards the West are exceptionally drunk, far drunker than I have seen them before. They seem to be celebrating the sale of a particular herd or a particular prize animal. The hammer and the trophy have changed ownership, yet the two men still sit drinking and leaning in towards each other whispering about further treasures. Leevee is joined now by his wife, Nell. She is so incongruously slim beside him that all I can think of when I see them standing in what seems to be a rather frigid proximity to each other is: their marital bed. She has short dark hair and white acne-scarred skin. She has grown into handsomeness and she is kind to me. Each morning she asks quietly if I have slept well and if there is anything I need to make my stay more comfortable. I tell her that everything is in order.

I gesture across the room to her for another whiskey. I have had four large glasses now and the same number of porter. None have dulled my anxiety. The whiskey is passable but this porter, though sweet at first, bloats me badly and gives me a headache.

Rhatigan stands at the door, frowning at the room. I can tell from his disdain that he views all drinkers as beneath him – puppets acting out a distasteful play. He sees me, and his face softens. He strides through the smoke and takes a seat, produces a cigarette and offers me one too. I take it and light it from his struck match. I find his hand cupping the flame, coupled with the way he stares with such intense care at the end of my cigarette, moving. I suck, and he pulls the match back towards his own cigarette, sucks, then shakes it out and mutters, 'Christ, I haven't been in this place for a while.'

'I decided to take a drink,' I say.

'No harm sampling the local fare,' he replies with a smile. 'Little else to be doing out here I suppose.'

'I talked with that man at the bar,' I say. 'The museum owner, Shaihmeen ...'

Rhatigan shakes his head, 'French? A museum owner? – ha!' Then, looking at me and perhaps seeing that I find all of this plausible, he continues, 'Well, okay, now you say it, I suppose it is a museum of sorts. He collects and sells and collects to sell again and collect, and if that's not a museum owner then I suppose, yes ...'

'He invited me to visit.'

Rhatigan's eyebrows raise as he smiles once more. He seems impressed that I've gained an invite from this Shaihmeen French.

One of the wealthy farmers at the turn in the bar falls with a thud from his stool. The other three guffaw as they lift and right him. He winces and puts a hand to his hip. Rhatigan peers at Leevee then at the flailing group of farmers, as if by looking at them in this way they will bring themselves into order.

'Gombeenz.'

I know only from the way he says this word the meaning of it.

I take a sip from my whiskey.

'Would you like to join me in a drink, Gunter?'

I make to stand, but he puts his hand gently on my arm and shouts to the bar, 'Leevee! A lemon cordial there.'

Leevee nods as he cleans a glass with a frayed tea towel. Nell moves to the other end of the bar and prepares Rhatigan's drink. Leevee swivels, bends and turns a radio player on, and some moments later shreds of crackling orchestral music drift up into the light-shafted smoke. This music goes unnoticed by the other men who are all now deep in close and excited conversation.

I tell Rhatigan about the policeman's visit, to which he nods. Then, taking another draught from my whiskey, I inform him of my letter.

He looks to me and says, 'And this would be of concern to you?'

'It is,' I say, 'very much so.' To this we fall silent, and from this silence I begin to tell him about my mother and how when I was young she used to play chess against my uncle for hours at our kitchen table. She beat my uncle often, despite him being a candidate master and one of the finest chess players in Kazan. Then, after she died, I tell Rhatigan, I used to take her chessboard and her old sewing materials, too, and I would sit with these things at the kitchen table. I'd open the board out to ninety degrees, pierce holes with needles through the squares where my mother would once have placed chess-figures and I'd guide lengths of thread through these holes, and, using these tautened threads of various colours, the chessboard panels would be held agape. 'Not dissimilarly to how a pop-up book of lines, planes and Platonic solids might work,' I say. Then, I tell Rhatigan that through my teens I'd collect more and more chessboards and develop in these chessboard-spaces increasingly complicated systems for illustrating shapes meeting each other, or interpenetrating, until, almost unknown to me, I'd developed an aptitude for visualizing geometrics of a very complicated kind. Then, one day I brought one of these 'pop-up books' into college to show a visiting lecturer, Rogkov, what I'd meant the day before when I spoke about the 'trigonometry of feint, capture and play', and he, looking on at these multi-coloured networks of taut thread in the chessboard I'd opened out before him, asked after my name. I said, Lobachevsky, to which his mouth fell open, and it was from this moment, I tell Rhatigan, who listens to me patiently, that I was elevated by Rogkov towards the world of Soviet mathematics where a film of protection began forming around me, and with this I was and have been forgiven any small transgressions or perceived transgressions on my part simply because of the great use I might become to the state, but, I say to Rhatigan, I never developed into the mathematician I promised to be and instead have since received posts of decreasing responsibility, and this is why I am concerned, I say, while sipping my whiskey, after five slow years of quietly but consistently displaying my lack-of-value to the state and its leaders that the time has perhaps finally come for any transgressions from my past to be stacked against me and counted up.

Rhatigan looks away. After some time, us both looking on at the other captives in the bar, he turns to me and asks what I will do.

'I cannot return, Gunter,' I say, 'that much I know.'

I drop my head. I can feel the alcohol. I then feel his hand on my shoulder as he lifts himself to produce from his pocket a tin of snuff. I decide to bring this part of our conversation to an end and console him and perhaps myself by suggesting that I might have connections in London to whom I can write and, I tell him, that they will advise me on what to do.

An hour or so later and it seems that everyone in this bar has migrated towards Rhatigan and me. People in this locale seem to gather around him: even if he enters a room alone, soon one, then two, then three people will have drifted into his orbit. Some days I can feel this pull myself.

Our conversation has dried up into the raised voices of the men around us. I've spent these quiet heady moments gauging the other end of the bar as a suitable space to host a set of geometrics that I can use to illustrate to Rhatigan the wavering bogland upon which we have struggled for the last number of weeks. I want to communicate the problem to him using line and form and to see how well he enters this game. I invite Rhatigan to join me away from the din.

I remove from my satchel the ribbon, string, wool and rope. I ask Rhatigan to sit beside the smouldering fire as I stand on a stool and tie one end of a length of blue ribbon to the curtain railing above a window. I run this ribbon down to the leg of a high stool at the end of the bar, until it pulls tight. I take a second length of blue ribbon and loop it around a wall lamp a metre to the right of the window, and draw this ribbon down to the same point on the leg of the stool.

'Can you see that inclined triangular plane?' I ask.

Rhatigan nods. Behind me French stands, and his tall and slim friend, now swaying beside him, steps into my arena. I ask him to please stand back out. I walk under the blue triangle and heave the window up. Cool air courses in, dispelling smoke. Leevee appears at the turn in the bar. The three wealthy farmers still laugh at the other end. Their friend sleeps on the couch behind. I produce from my satchel two lengths of yellow rope. I bid French to hold the ends of these ropes as if they were the reins of a horse. Then I ask his tall and slim friend to go outside and come to the window. He looks at me in that amused way heavily drunk men sometimes do, then leaves. Moments later he appears at the window. I hand him the other ends of the yellow ropes and direct him to back away until the ropes tauten. A few moments later I hear him knock over what sounds like a bucket. The yellow ropes slacken, criss-cross, then go parallel and taut, and with this enters into the room too a strange feeling of tension.

French looks at Rhatigan who is looking at Leevee who is looking at the three drunk and wealthy farmers now gathering somewhat menacingly at the turn of the bar. One of these men says, in a way that is more cough than question, 'Fuck's this.' I fear they may destroy my illustration.

I hear the radio music through the near silence, a lifting aria, and I imagine an opera singer's spotlit face, elated, on a stage in a city somewhere east of here, calling out towards a firmament of notation achingly far above her. I ask the three surly farmers to come to the blue triangle and I hand them each a piece of red string. They are for a moment disarmed and in this calm I ask them to hold their ends to the points of the inclined triangle. Two stand on squat stools and put their strings to a vertex each, while the third farmer lies on the ground, as if he were slipping underneath an auto to repair a leak, and holds his red string to the point on the leg of the stool. He is laughing wheezily, his eyes tearing up.

I ask Leevee to sit on the stool. He emerges from behind the bar and descends onto the stool with a creak. No one utters a word and I realize the form taking shape has begun to replace their doubt with curiosity. I pull the three loose ends of the red strings towards the centre of the blue triangle until they meet and go taut. I ask Rhatigan to remove the shade from the table lamp and to lift the lamp over these intersecting strings. I think of my mother's sidelong look from her propped chin as she played chess against my uncle, her calm face, her darting eyes – as if viewing a great tragedy unfolding far below. I take a piece of pink wool from my pocket and hand it to Rhatigan. He hands me the lamp in return and I direct it over the converging red strings at the centre of the blue triangle. Without instruction, Rhatigan hunkers and goes to where the shadows of these red strings intersect on the floor and he pins the length of pink wool to this point with his finger. I release the three red strings and they fall towards the farmers. I lift the other end of the length of pink wool Rhatigan has pinned to the floor and pull it though the centre of the inclined blue triangle until this string is perpendicular to the plane. I ask Nell to turn off the lights, and in the darkness I move the lamp Rhatigan handed to me not moments ago around this large cat's cradle of wool, ribbon and rope and these elements throw themselves as line- and curve-shadows out across the walls, across transfixed faces, the windows and the umbrageous smoking fireplace. The line-shadows strike the corners of the room, breaking into many angles. I move the lamp around once more until the shadow of one line falls diagonally across Rhatigan's face; it runs up his chin across his lips, his cheekbone, his eye socket and into the pupil of his left eye where it bends and disappears, travels into a dark plumbless eternity, only for it to reemerge moments later over the rim of this pupil, up past his eye socket and over his raised eyebrow, his forehead and onto a branded wall mirror behind. I call towards the open window to the tall and slim man in the courtyard and ask him to whip his yellow ropes into waves, but I can see now the ropes have gone limp and that he has either fallen asleep or has silently disappeared home into the night. One of the wealthy farmers wobbles, then plummets from his stool. He yanks with him a side of the blue triangle and with it the curtain railing shears from the wall. This overweight man lands face down, smashing onto a table full of glasses. Figures spring towards him as all the once-taut and beautiful lines collapse in their wake. Spinning shards of clear and coloured glass fly, flash and skid across the puddling floor. Rhatigan catches this large and inebriated farmer by his shoulders before he slips from the table to the ground. The farmer, though, has already sliced his cheek open on a piece of glass and his face is bubbling with blood. Leevee leans forward, pushes a towel to the farmer's stubbled face and he asks Rhatigan to 'call the vet Ohaarah. This lad'll need a stitch'. I step back, and for a moment this shadowy scene of men surrounding another fallen man prints itself onto my retinas; then, the music disappears and the fluorescent lights overhead come up, razing all of the shadows.

I can see French has already begun reeling my ropes in through the window, like a fisherman at the end of a disappointing day at sea. The strings and ribbons have been pushed asunder and my colourful proposition has been destroyed before it was complete. French hands me the balled-up ropes and I linger for a moment, hoping to catch Rhatigan's eye to see if he has understood the problem on the bog, but he has already disappeared to the telephone box in the forecourt to call the veterinary surgeon.

3

I wake dry-mouthed at some moment in the blue of dawn to Leevee's wife, Nell, naked and standing at the end of my bed. Her breasts are small, her nipples hard and her skin grey. She, wide-eyed, looks down at me intently. I shake my head with a seriousness I have not felt before. I put my hand to my head, rub my eyes; then I look once more. Leevee's wife, Nell, still stands there. Smiling, she lifts her hands to her eyes and acts out a peek-a-boo motion three, four times.

4

Rhatigan steps from his auto and leaps a gate to a grass-and-gravel track arrowing into a dense forest.

I can tell that he is frustrated, furious. The reserves of surveying stakes have not been replenished. It is Friday, in the late afternoon, and we are still two linear miles short of the obelisk beside the power station. Rhatigan had left Fvinegin, a broad-shouldered and bald man with what might be called an open and friendly face, in charge of keeping the surveyors in sufficient stakes, but this Fvinegin was elsewhere when the timber merchant last visited their office.

I leap the gate also and follow Rhatigan as he stomps into the forest. It lies three fields to the north of the shores of a lake and in the middle of this forest of ash and oak, I've been told, lie two acres of softwoods, and in the centre of that a man they refer to as Klanzci runs a tree-felling business.

It has begun to rain heavily after what was a pleasant morning. Symphonies of papping sounds fall from the broad leaves overhead. What is left of my drink-headache is passing, leaving only mild fatigue. Rhatigan has mentioned nothing to me of the hotel lounge from the evening before, nothing of my troubles, nothing of my illustration.

In the clearing before us, Klanzci and a young boy, whom I assume is his son, are dragging the bole of a conifer tree across a concrete yard. Behind them stands a shed and beyond looms a corrugated building that must be their store, all framed in the green of towering pines. Smoke drifts from the clattering splitter, up into the now dispersing rain. Klanzci, a red-haired man in his thirties, with arms that seem too long for his body, turns, and upon seeing Rhatigan drops his end of the tree and indicates to this blond young boy to strip it of its branches. The boy picks up a large-toothed hand saw and begins sawing at the branches of the tree. He does this with such unselfconscious skill that he resembles an experienced farm labourer handling an enormous sheep.

Klanzci looks to me, but Rhatigan does not introduce us.

'Bit of a crisis, Bobi,' says Rhatigan. 'We need a hundred stakes by tonight,' and, stepping closer, he continues, 'I've to report to Dublin by the end of next week. They're like bloodhounds on a fucking leash.'

'Christ,' replies this Klanzci, and they walk towards one of the large buildings to the end of the yard.

I look on at this blond youth cutting and snapping the last branches from the bottom of the tree trunk. He summons me to help him lift it onto the cutter. Together we drag the length of conifer up onto two thick steel Vs extending from a considerable set of metal legs. From the end of them we shove the bole a half of a yard beyond, and together saw it off. We lift this wet half-yard of timber and set it upright onto the steel table. The boy revs the canting chopper, swings its arm into place above the timber and releases the brake. An axe descends onto the top of the gnarled trunk. Its heft halts the blade for some moments until the young boy revs the machine further and the axehead eases down into the grain. The bole groans, squeals then splits in many directions until a seam opens up inside the trunk into which disappears the axehead. The timber crackles like the spitting of a deep if distant fire. The boy puts the engine into reverse, lifts the blade out and swings the arm in an oily rattle away. He topples two halves of this half-yard of tree off the table and nods to me. We set one of the halves of this wet conifer upright upon the table and the boy sends down the blade once more. I think for a moment of Gusev. I picture him in a threadbare quilt coat and felt boots standing next to a stack of giant tree trunks covered in snow, on the edge of a vast tract of felled forest, with receding brick chimneys issuing opening knots of blue-grey smoke into the air. It is early morning, before dawn, and he is shivering. His eyes are dark and trained emptily on the ground before him. He steps towards me until he disintegrates.

The youth topples the lengths of timber off the steel table, turns to me and rubs his reddening nose, and I realize this boy has a cold and that he looks ill, short of iron, and probably should not be labouring in this way.

'We'll sort you boys out, don't worry,' he says, in an unbroken voice, thick with accent.

Rhatigan and Klanzci reappear, their arms filled with pale stakes. They drop them at the splitter and Klanzci gestures to the boy, who scampers off.

'Appreciate it, Bobi,' says Rhatigan as he advances past me.

I follow Rhatigan once more back down the track. His boots churn the gravel and the square tails of his blazer flap delicately behind. The tree tips, way above, wave and rustle in the brightening sunlight. As the trees thin, I glimpse the yellow fields of wheat and the white lake in the distance, swelling and twinkling. I want to tell Rhatigan about the first time I saw a man diving backwards from a lake and landing on a diving board. I want to tell him what a man looks like when he emerges feet-first from a splash in an otherwise peaceful body of water. It was in a cinema in Moscow almost fifteen years ago and I was with Gusev and Matvei on a weekend break from our camp. It was a film by our hero, Vertov, and was called *Kino-Eye*. It is a moment in the film that comes after footage of women and children labouring on a farm, cutting, then threshing, then bagging wheat. On their way home, all of these women and children stop at a lake and from an improvised diving board (an uprooted sapling laid across the forking branches of two large trees) they dive into the water and wash themselves before they continue home for their evening meal. After one boy dives into the lake, a notice similar to a news message fills the screen, announcing: 'Kino-Eye shows how one dives properly', to which the film cuts from the agrarian lake of these women and children's younger days to an outdoor pool, in some large town. The pool is walled off with great boulders, and from the diving board to the right of the frame a diver takes flight into an expert arc that ends with a splash, but the splash doesn't fully form, it stops and begins to implode, and then from this disappearing implosion reemerge the ankles, legs, buttocks, torso, head and arms of the diver, whereupon he re-describes his flight back to the diving board above the pool, where he appears to stumble for a moment before the film cuts once more.

I want to describe to Rhatigan how witnessing this man reversing from water to air had once stirred, recalibrated, feelings of love in me. I want to tell him how Gusev, Matvei and I had bent over laughing at this film on that magical day of break from camp. I want to tell him how Matvei's blue eyes streamed with tears in the quaking cinema light, and how afterwards we went for a coffee, and then to a lake ourselves. But instead I say nothing.

As we round a turn in the track, the steel entrance gate framing Rhatigan's black auto comes into view. A tractor rattles at speed behind us. It is the boy. He slows, and Rhatigan and I leap onto the trailer behind, which is strewn over with these stakes. I place my feet between two pairs, and feel them bob and bump against my ankles. We accelerate towards the gate, disembark and the boy kills the clattering engine – it falls into grunts, then hisses, then silence. He unlocks the gate and wordlessly helps us load the rear of Rhatigan's auto until it is laden with these freshly cut stakes. Using lengths of blue twine we tie the boot, but it will not fully close. Rhatigan is unpleased with such a solution. He stands over it a moment.

As we speed off, Rhatigan thrusts his hand out of the window and waves. I look back at the boy, but he is locking the gate. He leaps onto the tractor, shudders it into life, turns his torso and slings his head back in the manner of a labourer twenty years his senior. As he puts the tractor into gear I realize he is aiming to reverse all of the way back to the yard, and I realize too, as he disappears, that he is one of those sorts of children who intuitively know how to work machines. One could put him into an aeroplane as easily as into a tractor, as easily as behind a film camera, and he would quickly become comfortable controlling the horse-power these sorts of contraptions stow – he would bring these powerful machines under control in a way that I struggle to imagine.

As we turn from the trunk road leading east, and onto the poorly sealed road running past the burnt-down estate home, I notice Rhatigan has mellowed. His shoulders have dropped and he is smoking a cigarette. The greens of the hedges and countryside course past while he taps his fingers on the steering wheel to a melody, perhaps, playing some-where far off in his mind. As he pulls in and grinds the auto to a halt beside Kolim and Mehl, both of them rising from their hunkers, he utters from the side of his mouth, 'Another storm due here Sunday, Nikolai, but we should be well done by then.'

Grey plumes surge from the gravel as Rhatigan steps from the auto.

'Men,' he says, as they blink and wave the dust away.

By early evening we've left the bogland behind and have traced another two-thirds of a mile of equilateral triangles across the pastures. We are approaching the edge of the town of Gainston. Rhatigan looks to his wristwatch and reckons aloud that Klanzci will have delivered a proportion of the stakes.

'Mehl,' he says, 'we'll podge on.'

As they walk away, Kolim lies down onto the grass at my feet, puts his arms behind his head and makes to snooze. He is by far the calmest of these three men and I am unsure if this is because his friendship with Rhatigan is the most assured or if he cares least about Rhatigan's opinion of him. He is the least adept of the three in matters of technics, numbers and order. He is the one that follows rather than leads, but I think Rhatigan sees value in Kolim's mindset. I sometimes think he is either far cleverer than us or considerably more stupid. I can tell at least that he sees merit in us taking measure of this land in order to enable its use and not merely to apportion its ownership. He said something of this kind to me in a quiet moment one wet day soon after I arrived, while we were standing hip-deep in the middle of a lustrous field of yellow flowers not far from the cut-stone bridge from where we had set out, claiming that he would prefer the measurement of land to be carried out with the activities it can provide in mind, not to the metrics it revolts, he claimed, against.

I look down at him, his narrow face, his dark hair, the delicate folds of skin on his neck. I would guess that he has already fallen into an untroubled sleep in the dry and warm grass. After Mehl and Rhatigan have moved out of sight I pace for a while, then I lie down some yards away from Kolim's feet and look up at the sky. Clouds pass each other. Then one emerges from between two, like mist rising in the cleft of a mountain – hands shaping to pluck a difficult note on an upright harp.

'I heard about your performance down in Leevee's last night,' says Kolim.

In his drowsiness I can tell that he has something of a lisp.

'Did Mister Rhatigan tell you?'

'No, Mehl. He heard about if off Nell Leevee.'

I say nothing for a while and nor does he, and for a moment I wonder if he has dozed off completely. Then, I ask if he knows the chap called Shaihmeen French.

'What you'd call a tall-tales man,' he replies.

'He told me he owns a museum,' I say.

'He's a tall-tales man, Nikolai. I'd not believe a word out of him. He lives on his own on a holding by the Kljunbruni crossroads. A small well-run farm by all accounts.'

I fall silent and look once again at clouds drifting by, slowly altering in the electric-blue sky, a window in the painted ceiling of a dome of a foundation-less baroque cathedral.

'You know Rhatigan since you were young,' I say.

To which there is no response.

'I've learned his brother, Charles, died in an accident.'

'Car crash. Awful sad,' he replies with a strange finality.

'Was he similar to Rhatigan?' I ask.

'In what way?'

'Intelligent, decent.'

'He was more of the first and less of the second. Training to be a doctor. Awful sad.'

I pluck a length of straw beside me and pull the grains from its head.

'Are you enjoying this work?' I ask.

'I don't understand,' he says, 'why it's never close enough. Surely we could jimmy the numbers, and just get the thing going.'

I say nothing and within a few minutes I can tell that Kolim has by now certainly fallen asleep, as a gentle snore lifts out of the grass.

I put my arms out to stretch my chest, and my right hand falls upon a coat. In it lies something hard. I pull the object free. It is the yellow surveyor's notebook Rhatigan uses for recording the levels and angles of each stake. There are pages and pages of numbers. I flip through them until I realize that the 'comments' column to the right of the numbers is filled with writing more cramped and intense than the numbers populating the columns to the left. I look closer. These sections of notebooks of this kind most usually record details like temperature, time or physical features on the land – a tree, a lake, a rock – but here amid notes of these kind Rhatigan appears to have written verse, and in amid the doggerel he has written brief notes as to Colm's, Mel's and my 'state of being'. I realize how I had visualized their names as different to how Rhatigan spells them, and I wonder how differently then he and I must encounter and make sense of the rest of the world. As I read, it seems as if the physical markings on the land – 'burnt hazel stump, ringed in daisies' – become part of the verses, and the descriptions of our humours become reduced to mere arrows indicating up, down, across or diagonal, as if there is some swapping of humours between land and animal. I look to one of the recent dates and see two days ago my arrows go up, down, then finish, by the end of day, as an upward diagonal, similar to both Colm and Mel, as if we are weathercocks unknowingly displaying our moods. It seems while Rhatigan is taking measure of the land through the lens of the surveying equipment, he is also taking a measure of us, as if he might divine something secret in the land from how we behave on it. I notice then to the bottom corner of each page a small drawing. I flick through them, and for a moment the figures of three stick men themselves carrying sticks in their stick arms, with a hill framing them in the distance and a sun rising and falling behind, become animated. I flick through these sheets once more, gazing at the animation in the bottom corner. Then I put the notebook over my chest and close my eyes and allow the words 'breadth of tolerance' to unbind and rotate in my mind, words I've heard somewhere before and have held on to in the hope that they might make available to me some new terrain in which I might begin to understand more of Rhatigan. The sun comes out. I remove my spectacles and roof my eyes with this notebook. I too fall into a snooze.

I open my eyes to a dark blueness and to the sound of feet stamping across grass. Panicked, I grasp the land either side of me. Then I realize where I am.

Colm is already upright, brushing himself down and is facing Mel and Rhatigan as they approach, both carrying armfuls of stakes. They look almost jolly in the dusk.

'The more we get done before nightfall the later we can begin tomorrow,' announces Rhatigan.

They drop their stakes at our feet.

Mel runs his hand down his beard, collecting it into a point.

The tripod and theodolite is half a verst behind us, and needs to be swivelled around the last stake we drove into the ground so we can sling our triangles another mile beyond that, by which time we'll have almost arrived at the obelisk beside the chimney.

I hand Rhatigan his jacket and his notebook.

Within half of an hour we are back shuffling and hammering stakes into the ground. These men don't mind now that I help carry the timbers. In this clement weather my role as strict observer has morphed. The positioning of each stake is taking longer now, either because of the failing light or Rhatigan's tiring eyes. I walk towards the tripod to see, with the evening sun breaking through a row of poplars edging the field, what the visibility through the theodolite is like.

Rhatigan is adding numbers to the pages of his yellow notebook.

'May I please inspect?' I ask.

He nods, deep in concentration, calculating the levels and angles relative to the tripod. I lift my spectacles and lean in.

I see Colm and Mel standing side-on to each other, speaking surreptitiously, Colm gesturing with his thumb towards Rhatigan and me. Mel, waving a fly from his face, looks doubtful about what Colm has just said. He shakes his head. They step apart and then return as if to say something more, but bearded Mel then looks directly at the theodolite, his eyes burrowing into me. He holds his stare until it becomes almost unbearable to look at him any longer; then, I look to Colm who is also staring at me, expressionlessly, as if emptied of feeling, and it suddenly occurs to me, with a voiding certainty, that it was these two men who accompanied Rhatigan on the night he killed his brother. I look up from the theodolite, replace my spectacles, but by now the two men in the distance have drifted apart and are picking up stakes, and they seem to be smiling. I look down the theodolite once more and Colm is now peering carefully at me, back over his shoulder, and I reckon all that seems harmless in him is the precise obverse of what is pernicious, and I realize, if these two facets were the opposing faces of a larger complicated form like a dodecahedron, then what might the other opposing facets of this form comprise? What might the colour of these facets be and how best might one look on them, or through them or into them, and from this what might one learn as to the nature of the entity? As I step back from the theodolite I feel a shunt at my feet. I've trodden on one of the legs and the tripod has transposed.

'That move?' says Rhatigan.

For a moment I consider saying 'no'.

'It did.'

'Nik,' he says, peering up at me almost plaintively. I see him gauge me.

He lifts the tripod from over a small circle he'd beaten into the ground and takes another nail-shaped object out of his coat pocket and hammers it into the soil a few yards to the right. Cows in the next field low. Birds scatter, and in the distance more, in a gathering murmuration, pass in silent shadow-throwing curves and waves. He spends some moments centering the theodolite again. I move to one side as he squints down the lens at the last stake we hammered into the ground. He makes a note of this angle in his book, checks through the lens once more, then looks back to his book again.

'Only at half-mast today, Nik.'

'I was weary earlier.'

'That'll be the drink,' he says.

'One can have interesting thoughts while drinking too,' I say.

'Can one, now.'

I return to Colm and Mel, who are smiling cryptically, and I pick up the twenty-two yards of chain and walk out with them to a point in the field. By now we've become so accustomed to walking and turning at this twenty-two yards that we seem to do it in unison. It is an unspoken rhythm I won't easily forget and will most probably only ever associate with these fields and these two unnerving men – a chain of walk, with a type of precision outside of links and numbers.

It's dark by the time we leave for Rhatigan's auto. We fell three fields short of the power station, but Rhatigan was pleased with the progress, 'all the fucking around considered', he said. Over the last number of weeks it has given me pleasure at the end of each day to look back over our stakes rumbling across the land behind us. My life in recent years in the State Geometer's Office had filled with tasks of increasing irrelevance, and this walking and pulling and carrying here has tired and elated me.

As we march along the shadowing road, all I can hear are our clopping footsteps, the creak of the tripod on Mel's shoulder and the clink of the yards of steel that loop between my hands. Two cuckoos issue, from somewhere to my left, two descending calls. I can feel the cool twenty-two yards of steel in my fists and I wonder does each fist now carry exactly eleven yards. Mel walks behind me and Rhatigan and Colm are ahead with their hands in their pockets, chatting and laughing while they suck on their cigarettes. The outlines of their heads appear within a smoky orange halo each time they inhale. I can tell this is something they have done since they were young, walk a distance in the night, smoking a cigarette without removing it from their mouths – until it burns to the butt, and then spit it onto the asphalt below. It then strikes me that these men can see well into the dark.

In the auto on the way back to my hotel, Rhatigan tells us that 'we'll go again at dawn tomorrow'. He tells me to be outside waiting at six. I step from the car and bid them good-night and wonder what they say about me as they drive away, if anything. It has suddenly become cold. I enter the hotel and see it is all but empty. Nell is wiping down the taps at the bar. She doesn't look at me or greet me as I pass.

5

Next morning, while waiting for Rhatigan to arrive, I pace over and back across the hotel forecourt, stamping my feet in an attempt to generate a degree or two of warmth. The dew-covered fields are dotted with livestock. Some are lying like sphinx, and around them others stand, issuing jets of breath into clouds of vapour. Behind them more lope away with a slowness that belongs as much to the hour as, I imagine, to this place. In the breakings of the mist to my right, a swathe of our stakes appear and disappear as they ride the undulations of land where the bog and swamp and pasture interpenetrate before the pasture relents and the land turns to mulch. The ground I can see is of the sort whose name alters with the seasons and the levels of the floating water-tables beneath.

I noticed while passing stool this morning that the blood, which has appeared regularly over recent years, has reappeared again. I was told by my physician in Leningrad that while the blood remains bright red there is little of concern, but if the blood turns dark then I should present myself to a physician immediately because the blood is coming from within. Perhaps it is the diet here, drying my anus and creating this pain.

It is almost seven o'clock before Rhatigan arrives. He tells me his car struggled to start, but that the rear is 'loaded up' with stakes. The fog on the carriageway, as we go, is at times still thick and deep. When we arrive at the last corner in the road, the chimney stack of the power station appears where the billows of mist part – a mountain peak that has suddenly revealed itself to us.

As we drive I ask about the other aspects of the survey, and in particular the heights of the ground we measure at each point. I enquire if Rhatigan still hopes to run the two main drainage arteries along the miles-long lengths of our primary triangle, to which he nods pensively, saying, 'We may as well pull as much information at once off the ground as we can.'

Mel and Colm sit on the steel gate to the field we finished in the night before. None of the stakes in these fields has been touched. I consider them being left untouched on this land as a grudging show of local welcome to a new idea strong enough to offer deference.

Mel has a black eye and a cut to the right of his nose. Nothing is said about this to him and I can't tell if it is because such a thing happens so often as to be beyond comment or if these men would not bring such a private matter up for discussion in front of a visitor such as me.

'Two more stations, I'd say, and we're there,' says Colm, as we set out into the field.

By midday the sun has burned through the mist and we are gathered at the plinth of the power station chimney. Rhatigan sits forward in one of the German huts, calculating his entire triangulation. Above us leans the scaffolded-out beginnings of the station's turbine hall. Rhatigan steps from the hut, announcing that the triangulation is incorrect vertically by two inches over the distance of six miles. He seems to think this is acceptable. 'The problem, though,' he continues, 'is that the triangulation is out by almost a foot in the lateral direction …' He is biting his lip. I can tell he is not pleased. I sense Colm and Mel are not breathing. The thoughts of ripping up these stakes and starting again does not appeal to them. I cannot believe they have done this four times before I arrived. I know that if Rhatigan were somehow to fail here, then their sense of failure would fall much deeper, but only for a time, whereas his would stay hovering before him, taunting him until he had righted the world around it. I understand now the tension between them performing these measurements around their home with their neighbours and friends urging them on, or in front of enemies quietly wishing them ill. I think of Matvei at a lake, on a bright day, swinging on a rope out over the shining shallows, then unhanding the rope and plunging into the water with a splash and a cheer.

Rhatigan looks to me, 'Any ideas there, Nik?'

I saw this once in Kirov: an old surveyor called Burkov, who was struggling with lateral tolerances on a project, sent fifteen men out into the bogs around us with fifteen bags of six-inch nails, fifteen hammers, fifteen spirit levels and fifteen knives.

'We'll improve the lateral tolerances at each stake,' I say to Rhatigan, 'if we split the triangulation into four; each of us take a spirit level, a sack of flat-top nails, a hammer and a knife. We hammer a nail into the middle of the top of the stake, then level the stake with the spirit level, then scrape an X into the top of each nail, then re-survey the whole thing again, but instead from the more-precise centres of these Xs.'

Colm and Mel look to Rhatigan.

He is staring at me with what might be termed admiration. A trickle of molecules recollect as his looking into me recedes. He rubs his face – his fingernails dirty with gatherings of peat.

'Hmmm,' he says, smiling.

By five o'clock that evening we are walking with Colm as he finishes his last ten stakes. He is uncomfortable at us watching him carrying out his work. He is unsure of his method and he is not proud that we completed our parcels of stakes before him. Rhatigan follows, placing his spirit level to each stake Colm has righted. After each one he calls, 'Good man, Colm!'

Mel finds this increasingly funny. He looks hideous when he laughs – his right eye has blackened and closed half over.

He runs a hand across his sweating brow. The day here has slowly become stifling.

'What's happening now, Gunter?' he says, into the quiet falling between the timbers. And Rhatigan steps forward, a smile playing on his lips as he places his spirit level on the north, south, east, west of another of Colm's stakes. He stands, rubs sweat from his face, then pauses, and I see Colm ahead look forward and pause too. Gunter pauses further and looks at Mel, who is suppressing a laugh, and Colm, who is listening keenly, daren't turn around. Then Gunter emits once more: 'Good man, Colm! Another veritable North Pole!'

Colm continues, dolefully, with his levelling and hammering and his scarring of these Xs.

A number of stakes later, and Rhatigan's pause is so absurdly long that Colm is forced to look around. He sees Rhatigan and Mel with tears streaming down their faces, laughing soundlessly. He looks at me and sees that I am shaking with laughter also, and he says, 'Fuck you, Gunter, now, fuck ye all!'

Colm merely walks on, but his show of dignified gumption only makes the scene more humorous. The two men beside me bend over and release giant hoots. I've come to realize that Rhatigan plays these two underlings against each other with a gentle alternating of his favour. I do not doubt both of these men would like nothing more than to have Rhatigan for himself, and I realize in how they move around him that they aspire to what is in him that's capable of producing cruelty.

We arrive at the stone bridge and Rhatigan checks the last stake, which protrudes from the reed-lined bank some four yards short of the parapet.

The wind picks up as a creaking freight train eases by overhead. Its wagons are laden with creosoted electricity poles, hoppers full of anthracite and a flat trailer with stacks of red bricks covered over in sheets of black tarpaulin, ripped and flapping.

'Five miles an hour,' says Rhatigan to me in disgust. 'That restriction's been there a year. Do you know how much that sucks from the country?'

'We took a walk along it one of the days,' says Mel, burying his fingers into his beard, where he scratches at his throat.

He looks to Colm who appears relieved at not being stalked any more.

'A mile west and the sleepers have rotted through the middle. Either they don't know how or they can't afford to fix them ...' he continues, 'either way; 'tis cat.'

'Maybe they don't feel like it's theirs to fix,' says Colm.

Mel shakes his head with what I take as a mock-wistfulness. I am not always quite sure when these men are joking. He pulls a cigarette from his packet then offers us all a cigarette too, and we light and smoke together as the sweat rolls down our backs.

Mel, rubbing his armpit, exhales into the air, 'What do you think, Gunter? Will we start measuring back the way?'

'Can't wait till Monday?' says Colm, grinning.

'Christ no,' says Rhatigan, 'I want to test this Russki's masterstroke,' and he looks to me, then smiles, 'we'll go when we're fresh, tomorrow. Come; I'll drop ye all back.'

As we travel, the air becomes even more heavy, humid, and Rhatigan comments on how this storm 'must well be now brewing out West'.

6

I sit at my usual table in the hotel bar, having come down from my room. I've washed for the first time in days. They brought a jug of hot water up to me, along with a cloth and a bar of soap, with which I flannelled myself over the ceramic basin on the chest at the foot of my bed. I've ordered a whiskey and a sandwich, though I know neither agree fully with my stomach.

The clock over the bar dongs six times and one of the men at the other end of the room removes his cap and blesses himself. It's an unconscious gesture he has inherited from a long time ago, and I can't tell if it is the gesture itself or the unconsciousness of it that he was bequeathed. I have my notebook before me with the letter beside, having re-read it several times more to see if perhaps I am misreading it, or if this 'special appointment' might merely be referring to a giant palace project in Warsaw, mooted in our office years before. I push both notebook and letter aside.

Leevee and Nell are standing at either end of the bar. They do this often, fall into a trance together and gaze out of the front windows at the birds, the livestock and the rolling fields. Their building becomes a skull holding two eye-worlds far, far apart. Then someone enters and they are jolted from their trance. In those moments I often wonder, if no one ever entered this establishment, would Leevee and his wife ever come out of their trances.

'Walthur,' they say, redirecting their gazes to the door.

'Gentle folk,' replies this Walthur, a slight man with black curly hair and a pair of steel-rimmed spectacles not dissimilar to mine. The front door swings closed. I can tell he is not a local person as he walks to the bar and sits, or at least I can tell that his elders were not from here by the cagey warmth shown to him by the Leevees, who I surmise have deep family roots in this place.

'A big one coming,' he says. 'I was thinking I'd pedal out of the town for a change. They reckon it'll be the last one of the summer.'

'You can feel it,' says Nell, now fanning her face with a sheaf of pink paper tickets.

An hour later, in rush three men, as Leevee places candles and paraffin lamps around the bar. Rain splatters down outside. Puddles form in interlinked asphalt craters at the side of the road. The men had been riding from a dozen miles west. They say there is a dance in the town tonight, but they don't want to turn up 'wet as rats'.

I hear a rumble from outside and can see the dark clouds pouring through and underneath each other as if they are trying to somehow return themselves to the ground. The weather here at this time yesterday was so bright it is hard to imagine that place as this. The climate in this corner of the world seems to ask its subterranean citizens to reimagine themselves at almost every moment of every day. On the morning I first arrived in this country, I saw, on a desk in Dublin Port, the words 'No fixed abode' written on a ledger beside the name of a young woman, Hilde Gudrun. She sat nervously across from me in the customs office, waiting for her papers to be checked. On the most changeable and wild of days here I think of those words and apply them for moments to every person trapped navigating around under these changeable skies. A white-and-black dog wanders in. It is a skinny creature, soaking wet and shivering. Nell darts from behind the counter with a broom and chases it out. The dog shoots back through the swinging door and into the rain, with a lopsided gallop and a whimper.

Leevee lights a candle in the middle of the bar, then leans to his left and lights a lamp. This region of the county I've been told was one of the first places to be given electricity – to be 'switched on', as they describe it. Here, they tell me, sits within the constituency of the Minister of Defence, a Makiovn, whom, Rhatigan told me one afternoon, made his name canvassing these parts of the Midlands with a figure called Kolensz. Rhatigan then told me, laughing, that if Makiovn or Kolensz met with anyone who was wavering as to which side they should take, Makiovn would offer to wrestle them; and if the victor was he, then the wavering man would pledge allegiance to the cause, and if this Makiovn lost, which I believe was rarely, then the wavering man was free to choose to continue to waver or join the other side. This Makiovn, who stripped each time to his waist, won hundreds of wrestling matches in bars, farms, crossroads and fields, but now, according to Rhatigan, he is a senior minister in this country and he organized quickly, perhaps as a show of power, for his constituency to be 'switched on' before this part of the country was technically prepared for such developments. They ran a 200-volt cable down from a town they call Birr, twenty miles north of here, with the sole purpose of lighting up a few houses and businesses in Makiovn's rural districts. Leevee, a man of progressive mind, immediately connected up, and within a week I'm told he dismantled and sold his one-stroke wind turbine. Rhatigan drove me, on the afternoon soon after I first arrived – and mere hours after we had visited his old country school – to this town called Birr. We traced over the land this single electricity cable hanging from telegraph posts, newly erected electricity-company poles, the gables of hotels, substations, churches and houses until we arrived on the outskirts of Birr, where stood a steel mast, its arms akimbo against the grey of the sky.

'Our first pylon,' said Rhatigan looking out the window with obvious pride.

It stood glinting in the field, livestock motionless around its base, with this single electricity line leading up to and beyond it. We continued into Birr and stopped at the rear courtyard of an old British army barracks, which had been taken over by what they refer to as: The Rural Electrification Scheme. Rhatigan jumped out and was greeted with warmth by another Irishman to whom I was immediately introduced as 'this famous Russian geometer'. The man's name was Mahnkhyn and he in turn introduced Rhatigan and me to a small Italian man alongside him, called De Maria. Rhatigan asked if we could see the arrangements, and this Mahnkhyn, a tall man with broad shoulders and a well-worn tweed blazer, led us towards the cut-stone wall that ringed a yard where the British army had once practised their manoeuvres and marches. We continued up to one of the old army watchtowers, and across this vast courtyard below lay organized in clusters the many elements and joints of over thirty pylons. At the end of the barracks yard stood a single pylon, whose assemblage this De Maria had overseen. He was from the Italian company that fabricated the pylons and he was here to colour-code and organize all of the parts that the Irish government had bought. He soon realized, I was told, that the most foolproof way of doing this was to lay all of the parts out, like a giant jigsaw, upon this yard once devised for the destruction of other traditions, people and things.

A vast crackle comes from over the roof of the bar, as if the room above is hosting an electrical force of some chthonic kind. The whole hotel bar, though, has its attention drawn to the outside. Their necks crane skyward. I rise and walk somnambulistically to the window. The clouds are black, and as they roll into greater nebulousnesses of black and grey, they begin to make the sounds of giant barrels half-filled with giant stones, rolling down the sides of giant mountains. The lights in the hotel bar flicker. Salmon sink in rivers. Those peering out of the window look back into the hotel bar, then back out of the window once more. It is only now passing seven o'clock and yet it feels like twilight on a winter's evening in Kazan. Nell has lit a dozen and more candles and lamps all dotted around the bar. She has set a candle on my table beside my glass of whiskey and she has lifted my breadcrumbed plate away. This Walthur has joined me at the window. He says nothing until in the distance a giant silver prong emerges silently from the sky and bends downward to touch the earth. A few seconds later a thudding growl chases across the land.

'That's a big one,' murmurs Walthur. 'I hope there's no one caught out in it.'

The lights in the hotel bar go down and we are in near darkness, then they click on once more. I look to the field over the slim trunk road and see that a grouping of the beasts I spied earlier in the day are lying down again. Some, however, are bounding towards the centre of the field. The field dips and three or four of them disappear, then reappear as they struggle up out of the drop.

I look to the fields towards my right where the land slips between swamp and bog. I can see a segment of our finely ordered stakes rippling over the contours in the mid-distance.

More lightning reaches down from the sky. It is like a midwinter branch made of nothing but light, and I think back to the day I first learned the German word for branch: *der Zweig*. It was during that time in Leningrad while I was re-translating my great-grandfather's treatise on the geometry of curves and I got waylaid towards the meaning of the word 'two' when I realized that the German word for 'branch' stemmed, or at least appeared to stem from the word: *Zwei*. At the time I had developed a brief but intense interest in the English translations of the work of Stefan Zweig and during this I'd come upon a letter he wrote to his friend Jules Romains from the strange Germanic city of Petrópolis in Brazil, wherein he claimed that his feelings of great disillusionment at having been forced forever from his home in Austria had led to him being unable to identify himself with the person on his passport – he said in his letter that he could not identify himself as 'the self of exile'.

The sky rips open again, and for an electronic moment the place flattens completely, goes dark, and, in the next, the world we were inhabiting creaks back up into shape, as if nothing had happened. Strangely, this time the branch of light from less than a minute ago appears again in exactly the same shape across the sky. Another rumble, then comes another deep broad growl. The rain is falling so hard now that I believe the road and forecourt will crumble, fill with water then grow and surge in upon us all. The remaining livestock in the fields opposite have lumbered to the hedges at the perimeter. Walthur looks on wordlessly, his mouth is what one might call agape. Leevee and Nell are at the furthest window, their hands now touching, while all of the remaining patrons have crowded wide-eyed around the other. It is as if we are all clamouring to see into ourselves but we realize this is at once the only and worst vantage point for such an endeavour.

I look to the broiling sky, then once more to the earth.

I put my fingers to my lips. 'The nails.'

This Walthur looks at me.

I take my head into my hands.

A thump, a pause, a rumble, all seeming to have come from underneath. I look up and another silent many-fingered prong dips to the earth, now like a dislodged branch, tumbling from a distant tree. Instead of it disappearing, though, into some other dimension on the other side of the sky, it flattens back into ours and spasms across the bog. It spasms like a thought. It spasms again, and again, and with it comes a flash that cracks throat-like across the land. Everyone stares at these bizarre strobes of light, but I know that the stakes we've set out across this terrain and the secondary benchmark we were within inches of designating must surely now be obliterated. The clouds spin and speed over the part of the land where the bog becomes pasture, lake, swamp and pasture again. What they call 'whins' shiver, trees shake and the meniscus of the lake in the far distance simmers. From the passing clouds comes another rumble. I look west and behind the dipping ridge of greys and black appears the slightest blue-green sliver of sky that widens and reveals the outline of the hill below. A few errant flashes and thuds appear and fade and fall. Rain smashes down for some moments, relents, then heaves groundward once more. Out across the land to the right, the stakes are burning in the rain, like tiny matchsticks. Again, I bury my face in my hands.

'Queer that. Can you see?' says this kind Walthur.

'I can,' I say.

The rain is now back to spitting, but it is the sort of rain you get in this place, when the worst has passed, and the rain seems to be showing, in the way the darkness has lifted an increment, what is light-hearted in its nature, and this facet of its nature mocks the great seriousness with which the rain had fallen not minutes before. It seems to mock too our own quivering and quaking, which for even the smallest of moments in this strange part of the world can reach beyond the wettest parts of your person and leave droplets in the drylands of your soul.

The three men who entered half an hour before are preparing to leave. They are excited about this dance in town, but I no longer like to dance, and I have lost interest in women and men. I return to my seat and order another whiskey.

Leevee's wife, this Nell, as she delivers my whiskey, enquires if I am feeling okay. A short curving lock of dark hair droops down over her brow. She says I look 'ashen'. I am unsure what this means. She tells me it means that I look unwell. I tell her I am fine. I tell her that I am fine, considering. She does not quite understand what I mean by this, so she returns in silence to behind the hotel bar.

Within an hour I have left. The evening sun is illuminating the lower regions of the sky in a dark umber-and-lemon. The light is trying to carry this umber-and-lemon across the land but it falls short each time and what I am now moving through is the effort of this light. I traverse the empty trunk road and continue west towards the entrance to the service route into the bog. As I walk, the wind picks up and sends the gorgeous scent of water, bog cotton and peat rushing towards me. The sun is beginning to arc into the hill towards the west. Rhatigan told me one evening, while we were finishing our work on the bog, that on the longest day of the year, and if the weather is clear, the sun can be seen setting in a place immediately to the right of the base of the hill and then for the rest of the year its place of setting edges back up over to the left side of the hill, and by late winter the place of setting is then on the other side of where this broad hill meets the horizon, before the sun as it sets each day swings back the other way once more. I begin to smell damp smoke.

I do not venture far into the bog. In my headlessness I forgot to put on my work boots and I do not wish to destroy my only pair of shoes in this mud. I stand at the end of the service road and see that the damage is almost complete. The stakes, in as much as I can make out, are charred stalks, destroyed or simply no longer there. Even after an hour of walking, and with all of that rain, some stakes still flame. Some issue wobbling lines of smoke. I look as far into the distance as I can. A figure appears walking along the most remote edge of this bog. He or she shimmers, then stops, falls, stands, then turns to me. Who is this person? And why are they looking at me? With something like a gunshot sound or perhaps a last shred of distant thunder this figure disappears. The ground around me begins to fizz as if the bog water below is boiling. I leave as what I at first believe to be rain begins to fall, but when I look at my hands and then peer up into the sky I can see this rain is black and that I am standing in a falling drift of dark-brown and black snow. These globules of seared peat and water drift groundward for almost a whole minute until the place comes to rest. I hear the plaintive call of a single bird, and I wager with myself that it is one of those Kornkryaiks that Rhatigan mentioned to me one evening as we trudged back across this swathe of troublesome land.

Overnight, turning in my bed, I decide that I cannot bear to meet Rhatigan, Colm, Mel or to visit that part of the bog, where I imagine them, the next day, wandering around our scorched triangulations uttering the word 'cursed', or some word of that kind. I sleep; then wake late in the morning.

I borrow Nell's bicycle, and, turning from the hotel fore-court, I accelerate down the trunk road that brings me east. The day is dry and breezy. I cycle to the quarry and look upon the beginnings of a face of shining limestone emerging from what was once a natural outcrop of stone, weeds and moss. A number of weeks before, they exploded the first shard of limestone away. 'Falling flags of limestone,' they said in the front bar of the hotel. 'Flags,' they said, and I at first imagined slim lengths of limestone protruding stiffly from a pole as if the grey slate of stone were somehow the liveries of this region.

The quarry is still. The large grinder they transported here in parts over the previous three weeks is in mid-construction – an animal yet to know desire. Its metal feet stand in dark puddles. Rhatigan told me they want a whole concrete works established here for the developments across the bogland. He said they will 'chase the dark from the night of this country' as far west as they possibly can. He said they will 'chase it back out into the sea'.

A woman in a brown shawl wrapped over her shoulders and head ambles past. She has a strange forward-slanting gait. She bids me hello; her small head from underneath this considerable shawl nods two, three, four times as she passes. She must have descended on the path that winds up, around and seemingly over the lip of the quarry. I wonder how that first detonation must have felt to her. Did it pass up through her legs? Did she shake?

I walk my bicycle back to the crossroads and pedal up a broad hill, from the crown of which the land opens. Over my shoulder I look and I can make out the remnants of our frayed triangulations casting their useless dark dots across the terrain below. I turn back and speed off down the hill, where this road bellies and then flattens and the green hedges gather up either side of me. At the crossroads that leads to French's supposed museum I take the narrower road. Down its centre sprouts a line of grass from the poorly laid asphalt and gravel.

A small herd of large and healthy cattle approach from around the bend before me. A slap and a whoop echo from above the clump of hooves. French must be striding behind, tapping their hides with a stick. A dog bounds out from one side of the cattle, then the other. It disappears into a hedge, then reappears, barking. The herd comes closer and closer until they stream past me. I feel the odd bump and shove as their hot masses drift past, ribs, hinds, shoulders, lolling heads, swishing tails, a deep smell of flesh and faeces. An opening fist of flies blooms up from a dusty shaft of light below. French appears. I startle him. Then he merely looks unsettled and it strikes me he is not the kind of man that likes being looked at without his knowing, if even for the briefest of moments. Then – realizing I am unlikely to ever describe to others what he looks like when he is unaware that he is being observed – he softens.

'The Russki,' he says, bending his stick.

'Nikolai,' I reply, 'please.'

'You're lost.'

'I am not. I would like … I am here to visit your museum.'

He cackles.

'The divil got the better of ye?! C'mon here with me first. I've to leave these cattle above in the road field.'

I jump from my bicycle and follow French who in turn follows his swaying heifers and his playful and beautiful collie.

'We'll start with the house of lamps,' he says as he leads me towards a modest hut on the other side of his muddy yard.

The white and somewhat run-down house we passed at his entrance gate is where I assume he lives. It is a narrow thatched house with perhaps only a few rooms within. His yard opens out into another, covered over in mud shot through with hoofprints. On the islands of unmuddied ground, where I pick my steps, the surface of badly breaking concrete appears. The slab he poured here must have been far too thin and the grass and soil are pushing up through its flaws.

The hut is a small timber construction, painted over in creosote. He has built it up off six concrete blocks and it stands apart from another two huts, sitting parallel to each other adjacent to an old stone wall. What remains of this wall is falling apart and French has inexpertly patched it with more of this concrete.

He swings open the door and from behind it he drags out with the instep of his foot a large pale oblong of stone with a smooth semicircular indentation to the crown.

'A kwirin stone,' he says, 'one-hundred weight of a thing. I've the rest of it above at the house.'

'For grinding,' I say.

'Corn. Now that there's over two thousand years old,' and he looks at me, 'come in.'

There are three large tables placed along three of the walls. Through the window to the left spills daylight onto the curved shapes of a neat row of lamp heads sitting upon their gleaming brassy bodies. These objects are polished and perfect, and in front of them lies a box of matches beside an unused votive candle. On the table to the right, along the back wall, is arranged what looks to be a part of a dinner set. It is as if two persons later today might sit there, side by side, and eat their evening meal. Behind stand two Italian candelabras laden with tapered candles that have also not been used and to the middle of the table sits a pink porcelain house that looks to be of considerable value – a baroque table decoration, lost completely in time and lost more completely in space. To the right is another table full of objects I scarcely recognize. French can see me looking at the table, but he wants to take control of his tour.

'Big-house stuff there, we'll get back to that.' And he steps to the table of paraffin lamps. He lifts one of the glass heads, twists up a quarter-inch of wick, strikes a match and holds it to the wick until it takes flame.

He places the glass head back on and turns to me, saying with unambiguous pride, 'Everything in here works.'

The darker corners of the hut come up in flickers of amber.

'That's the parlour lamp there now, and beside it is a trap lamp and beside that a station-master's lamp,' he says, gesturing to a metal box with circles of glass in its faces. 'The parlour lamp,' he continues, pointing at a smaller lamp nearby, 'it was me mother's and the other two I bought off the Jonz's above in Kilaczii.'

I approach the table laid out in cutlery.

'From where did you get that table decoration?' I ask.

'Isn't it so well you saw that? That's from well east of here,' he says, leaning forward and brushing dust from its eaves, 'a Father Djun from Dublin brought that down to me one weekend. He'd got wind of a camera I'd come upon that'd been owned by a Father Maihunii, who'd used it to photograph Konolii on his deathbed.'

I know nothing of these people.

'And the priest offered me that house-chen as a swap. I could tell it was a piece of work, so I handed the camera over.'

'Where's it from?'

He looks at me over the rims of his glasses and shifts his weight.

'You know the church sheltered some strange folk here during the war. And that piece of porcelain was left by a Czech diplomat, who's since been accused of genocide beyond in Poland. He left that with the priest as thanks before he headed off to America.'

'Did the priest know of the diplomat's crimes?'

'I'd say he did. The house is worth far more than the camera. Maybe Father was more comfortable leaving something with that kind of badness in it here in a hut in the Midlands. Maybe he thought the evil would fall off it here in the middle of my not giving a flute,' he says, smiling.

The paraffin lamp emits a crackle. French rushes to it, lifting the glass head and quenching the wick.

'That glass'll break if it heats too quick in the damp,' he says to me, as if I did not know such a thing already.

Upon the surface of the next table are arranged six bronze pepper mills. They are onion-domed but otherwise of varying design, and are positioned on the table in a row, as if this is the beginning of an architectural layout for a boulevard of a new city planned for somewhere in the air between here and Dublin. Then, end to end, in a line to the front of the decorative mills lie three old tie presses – slim pieces of lacquered timber, brass-hinged, with a brass clip holding the pieces of timber fast. The first is red, the next a dark mottled blue with ornate corn-coloured hatching framing its edge. I think of my father's tie press in Kazan and I wonder where it might be now or if he has recently had reason to open it. The third press is softened around the edges. It is almost black and seems to be for a much larger type of tie. I can feel French look at me. I can tell he is interested in my being entranced.

'Sometimes I come down to this hut on my own at night and turn all of the lamps on and sit for a while in what's left of the dark.'

I imagine him sitting here among these things pushing against the great darkness outside, and I wonder what thoughts a man such as this might have in light such as that.

A cow in the distance lows into the convivial silence gathering between this French and me.

'That's the lamps,' he says, 'c'mon out to the next.'

We step down into the yard and as he walks in front of me I see he is trying to disguise a limp.

'The House of the Hammers,' he says cheerfully, gesturing forward, his cloth cap now pushed back on his head.

The two huts alongside each other are raised a block higher than the previous one. French has built two sets of steps up to the door of each; again with yet more of these simple hollow blocks laid unevenly upon each other.

The layout is the same inside: three tables, a short one to the right and to the left a square window admitting the afternoon sun. The first table holds more than two dozen hammers, and on the table in the centre lie arranged neatly another twenty.

'So you weren't joking after all,' I say.

'Why would I?' he says, closing the door we entered.

My attention is drawn to the third table, covered with seemingly random trinkets. I wonder how so random a collection of objects is permitted in so orderly a place.

'This one here is made with a length of leather,' he says.

'I can't thank you enough for preparing your collection for me like this,' I say, inadvertently interrupting him.

He stares at me a moment.

'It's always sitting ready here,' he says and he peers around. 'Now this is an interesting thing.'

He says each syllable of the word 'interesting' as if he has only just constructed the word for the first time. 'In-ter-est-ting,' as if he still finds the word itself of great interest. He holds the head of the hammer between us, and points at these compressed coils of leather.

'See now, that's a strip of leather rolled tight, with a set of screws put through it to hold the coils, and these then meet the handle. It's for beating sheet metal. You'd struggle to get that around here today.'

He passes me the hammer and I inspect it closely. I turn it in my hands then hold it to the light. The leading faces of the head of the hammer have been mushed by some years of use. I place the hammer down and pick up another. It is a large wooden mallet, but with a cylindrical head fixed again to a broad dowel of hard and polished timber. It's heavy. I mimic the movement of one hammering a sheet of metal.

'Were these used for types of roofing?' I ask.

But there is no reply. I turn and French is no longer there. I spin, look under the tables, look up, but … I walk to the door and find it locked. I rattle the door again. It is certainly locked. I go to the window and note there is no way to open it; it is but a plane of glass fitted into the timber wall. I rap on the glass a few times. It is too soon to panic, but I can make no sense of what has happened. Then the door unlocks, swings open and back in walks this French.

I look to him.

He looks back.

'Where did you go?'

'Nowhere.'

'What are you doing? I must now leave.'

'What's got into you?'

'You locked me into your hut.'

'This place is not locked.'

'It was. The door.'

He smiles. The sun plays on his glasses for a moment and I cannot see his eyes.

'Did you try the walls?' he asks.

'Why would I?'

I find his sudden crypticness irritating.

'Well, you'd have found this, dear Russki,' he sings, as he slides a section of the wall to one side revealing the inside of the neighbouring hut. He begins to laugh.

'Why would you do such a thing?' I ask.

But he still laughs as the sun falls into shade. He puts his right index finger in behind his glasses and rubs his jaundiced eye.

'Are you mad?'

'Maybe I am,' he says, shrugging, 'but that's what you get for sneaking up on me.'

I am surprised he would admit to his having been caught unguarded.

'You are mad,' I say.

'Maybe, maybe,' he replies, looking around.

He sniffs, rubs his nose with his cuff. His shoes scuff and squeak the floor. Then he makes to put his hands into his pockets, pulls them back and crosses them on his chest, 'But have you seen a museum like this before?'

'I have not.'

'Well then.'

'Well then indeed,' I say, now smiling, 'but I request that you please stay where I can see you; disappearing in a room full of hammers!'

He laughs again loudly – disproportionately loudly.

He relents and gestures, 'What do you make of that table … that's the brother's stuff. I kept some of his things.'

I look across its surface. A packet of matches; a box of cigarettes, Woodbines; some blue shotgun cartridges arranged upright in a circle; a metal crampon for snow; a school copybook covered over with tan wallpaper; some coins; a globe so out of date that it shows the extent of the Austro-Hungarian empire; a horse's harness; a tin flask for brandy; a damaged set of playing cards; and a tiny timber box, which looks like a cigarette holder. I open it and from the base of the case floats out the most delicate chime – a kind of lullaby, but I can hear the gears of the tiny barrel organ within grind behind the music. I close the box, but French has already entered the next room. He stands in there with his hands on his hips and proclaims, 'Toys and tools!'

I wanted to ask him about this brother, but all I can do is follow him into the room. To the left stands a table and beside the front door, a large and simple-looking wheelbarrow.

'You can pick out one toy, and I'll tell you about it.'

I stand to the table and survey its strange landscape. I spy an odd object to the rear. It's a piece of painted steel, cut into an outline showing Little Red Riding Hood and the Wolf with a toadstool sprouting from the ground between them. French, following my gaze, lifts this piece of steel off its plinth.

'There's a world of engineering in that,' he says, with the first of what I detect as being reverence, 'made by a prisoner of the fourteen-to-eighteen war.'

He lifts the pressed metal plinth out too and sets it down on the front of the table. He points to the underside of the sheet of painted steel and says, 'That's a six-inch nail, flattened and bent into those teeth.' He places the object on its prongs and lets it swing over and back. The window and the whitened light behind it throws the beautiful painting work into shadow. French points to the counterweight arcing like a sickle underneath: 'That's an unspent bullet. He must have been sweaty-palmed welding it. A madman, whoever he was.'

I look on at the thing swinging there. French shifts his feet, rubs the table and some particles of dust spiral upwards. A cow lows again, but from a greater distance. It lows six times; then, the place falls quiet aside from the creak of this toy.

'They're the things that are worth collecting,' he says, pensively. 'You'll never see them again.'

He turns, but I am held looking on at this wolf and girl swinging over and back, spinning out strange forces. I try to think of what these forces and suggestions of forces are but they become so intertwined, interrelated and independent at once that I seem for a moment to enter a state beneath trance, and I realize that here in this tiny hut on this quiet and filthy farm is the first time I have certainly seen art.

French is outside again. He stomps out of the doorway, bouncing down the steps his wheelbarrow of sticks and shovels. I turn from this swinging toy and see that he, framed by the door, is now standing in the yard, ankle-deep in mud, brandishing a sheep hook at his side, and he looks at me from some new depth in his eyes and calls, 'Come out here now, you Commie bastard, kneel before me and beg forgiveness!'

I look to the hook above his head and I am astounded at how narrow it is. I cannot believe such a thing could be slung around a sheep's neck in its moments of greatest peril. I feel the constriction such a thing would bring. I step forward and out of the hut and breathe in the farm air.

French has replaced the hook into his barrow and is now holding aloft yet another object. 'An eel-skin flail,' he says, smiling in the sun, 'an in-ter-est-ing thing ... for the thresh-ing of corn.' And he prepares to swing it over his shoulder.

But I shake my head. I've had enough and I realize if I don't stop him we will be here talking about his objects for days.

'I need a cup of water,' I say. 'I'm thirsty.'

I am surprised to see French's house is also with electricity. He seats me on a timber bench alongside his kitchen window. A glass milk churn stands in the centre of the table, its rotor-like blades upside-down within. I can't tell if French is repairing the churn for his collection or if he uses it every day. The 100-watt bulb overhead throws out light that does not quite suit the surroundings. It is as if the natural dirt of the place belongs to a natural kind of light and shadow too.

'You're obviously the type of citizen who might vote for Makiovn,' I say, pleased I can use this casual localism.

'I'm not. They're nothing but thugs. I can see the merit of the light, though.'

French fills an ancient-looking kettle with water lifted with a blue jug out of a chamber to the side of his stove.

He puts the kettle down on the stove, takes two enamel cups out of his cupboard and places them with an awkward bang onto the table. The cupboard door remains open and from it surges the scent of semen, faeces and meat. My eyes water and I ask what is producing that stench. He turns to me and laughs, then opens the other door of the cupboard and there hang six black lengths of dried meat.

'Calves' penises, curing, for the hound,' he says, and he closes the doors over.

He swirls warm water from the kettle into a small red pot, then he pulls a tin of what I presume to be tea from a broad shelf beside his cupboard, lifts the lid and tips some of the tea leaves into the pot. His now fluid movements, with the gentle clangs from these utensils and implements, make the place sound like a small forge near day's end.

He reclines with a sigh onto a tidy armchair facing his range.

'The museum,' he says, wincing, as he rubs his knee, 'it's made up of things I've bought, stolen, taken on loan or inherited. What I used to value most were the things I'd inherited from my father, my mother and the brother. But more recently I've come to treasure the toys.'

All of a sudden he seems to have aged well beyond his sixty-or-so years.

He stands and lifts a bottle of whiskey from the shelf above his range. He smiles toothsomely at me as he squeaks the cork off and pours whiskey into our cups; then, he sits.

I ask how these objects might be arranged after he passes on.

'Doesn't bother me,' he says, peering down at his neat feet. 'I just like telling the stories behind them. They'll fall dead I suppose once that part of them dies, when I die, and sure then someone else will make stories up about them and on they'll go making stories until the things disintegrate or fall out of favour.'

The water in the kettle begins to boil. After two attempts French heaves himself from his creaking chair. A clock in the next room chimes seven times. I wonder as to the grandeur of its surroundings.

I tell him about our problems measuring the bog. I tell him about our destroyed stakes.

He responds, as if in answer to the pointlessness he sees in our endeavour, with a description of the various colours the wind possesses here, and how from certain ordinates the colour comes in differently on the air. He tells me, as he pours steaming water into our cups, that around the Midlands these colours all mix to white if you think of the colours as light, or dun, if you think of these colours as pigment. Realizing that he has nothing of use to say about our problem, I tell him about my letter and about the upsetting dream I had the night before of three men gathered around the foot of my bed. To which he says a mere 'Oh.' But I can tell he cannot advise me on what to do, as if such advice would have consequences that he wants no part in, and I then realize how gentle a life it is he leads here. Instead – after reclining back into his seat, his cup in both of his hands – he begins to tell me about an island in the Tshanon estuary where his brother lost his life bringing seaweed back to the mainland. He tells me I won't learn anything new in Leevee's nor will I teach them anything new either, especially not with the sorts of games I was playing with rope and ribbon 'up there those few nights ago'. I can tell he found how I'd behaved distasteful, showy or simply unsatisfying. I understand from him speaking like this that in this place images do not come from pictures, or the shape of what is illustrative in pictures, but that images come from words and that fleeting images of this kind are a private thing. He tells me then as we drink our whiskeys-and-tea that there is a wind-like drift to language on this island where his brother perished, from the strange to the fitting, and that the people on this estuary island know this language of movement and uncertainty more intuitively than here, in the bog. Then, before I finish my whiskey-and-tea and leave him in his kitchen for the evening, he says that it was this interest in the language of movement and this un-suredness that kept his brother for so long away from the Midlands, and despite what befell his brother, he reckons, it might still be an interesting place for a visitor such as I to see.

PART II

Spinning circle passes spinning triangle.

1

I'm standing beside the well to the front of the small sand-stone schoolhouse. Children play in the yard behind. It is a bright day in mid-March and the estuary that yawns peace-fully towards the sea is, at this moment, barely moving. The air seems more full of salt than usual. I can taste it on my lips. The receding white tidelines in the distance interchange, disappear, and the occasional gannet or seagull floats up from the shore. This well is over sixty feet deep and its water is heavy with lime. When I arrived here first I was told: 'You'd only take a cup or two of it at a time.' I drink several cups of this water at the end of each day when I fill my pail before returning to my house, over the largest hill on the island, to prepare my evening meal.

The school bell rings and the screams of the ten or so children alter, then become muted, and I can hear their foot-steps slap and funnel across the yard towards the entrance.

Seagulls call overhead, while their shadows flit in runes along the ground.

I scan the seawater once more. I've done this every day since I've come here, checking the rolling land below me, waiting, with my heart tightening, for a strange approaching boat or a clutch of army officers or policemen in a vessel, indicating to me that I might at last have been found.

I shake out my cup and put it into my bag, step from the well and descend the steep syncline of this overgrown and grassy hill. The wind whips up and I feel my hair flail around upon my head. The grass chases up the incline in waves, bringing with it the scent of sea near land. Then it all falls into calm.

In the distance a large oily mound of black floats down the estuary. As this rick of seaweed turns in the water, two oars appear from either side. It's quiet Peter Guinane in his gandalow, bringing his haul to the mainland. This floating Guinane is one of four farmers on this island. I work for them all whenever they harvest their segments of foreshore. I've managed to organize my periods of work with these people well. The other three farmers are called versions of Guinane: Guinan, Guineáon, Geenaun. They've been on this island for centuries, each family a decade or two longer than the other. They joke often about who the rightful heir to the place is, and which of their names is a pun or a deri-vation or an amalgamation of the others. I like working with them all. Their methods for harvesting seaweed have little to no variation, but the parts of the foreshore they work from are so different, and their families so unalike in nature, that some days when I start with a new family I feel as if I have travelled a great distance to be with them.

I live on the northern edge of this island of barely 300 acres, amid the hedges and pastures, in a gatehouse once owned by a member of what they call 'the landed gentry'. He was a Colonel Jones, Lieutenant of Longford, who fought and lost a limb in India, or so I've been informed. His large many-windowed house lay empty for decades and is now a roof-less glass-less ruin, into which the islanders still do not venture. This gatehouse that I lodge in, though, remained intact. It sits in from the only road in this place, a narrow strip of unsealed asphalt that runs north to south up over a hill called Knok Moohr – the big hill. They call this place 'The Island of Four Hills', Ijlion Kahra-knok, but I can only ever count three, and when I pursue them for an answer to this inconsistency they laugh me off, saying that I am not looking hard enough, and they dismiss me as 'the crazy Pole'.

I spent all of last week with Guinan and his family harvesting weed in from their bay. Guinan was the first person I met here the day I stepped from the boat. It was a choppy morning and I'd vomited three times over the side of this vessel, owned by a small and sullen fisherman, it chugging down the estuary at high tide. He said his boat had too deep a hull and if we left our trip too late we'd be stranded on the shallows of the estuary for hours. When I lurched from the boat, with my bag over my back, I leaned forward once more and threw up onto the broad blue stones of the quay. Then, as I stood, there was this Guinan – a tall handsome bald man in a wind-bitten shirt and a pair of shining oilskin trousers tucked into two dark boots. He thrust out his enormous hand.

'I'm here for some work,' I gasped.

'You can work for me,' he replied.

I wave at Guinan and his son, Paulie Óg. They stand on the edge of the stone harbour looking over and back between the hill I descend and the gently heaving sea. Paulie Óg, an athletic young man with brown curly hair, whom I imagine is almost twenty-five, doesn't travel to the mainland anymore. He was in a love with a young woman there for years until she decided to go to the city of Limerick to become a teacher. He told me he had been 'courting' her, but that he was more serious about it than she and this seriousness led to an impatience in him, from which she apparently fled.

These two men wave back at me in that half-dismissive way that the people on this island tend to. I've made this trip with Guinan countless times. Today, though, the gandalow looks heavily laden. We are boating across to the small town of Motebeg approximately eight knots away. A farmer, Kriin, will meet us there to purchase the top third of our load as fertilizer for his small holding further inland. Guinan tells me this Kriin lost his segment of foreshore when forced to sell his 'low field' to a prosperous landowner from the east. He said it was much more than the field this

Kriin lost; he lost an ancient foothold in his country too. The remainder of the load we will float further up the estuary to the Kindara Alginate and Iodine Industries. Their prices are better per pound, I'm told, but Guinan can't bear to leave this Kriin short.

I step down onto the harbour as Paulie Óg stacks against the sea wall three wicker baskets alongside three crab traps. Guinan's mound of seaweed bobs at the foot of the landing. Its strange mossy tang surges up from the water slapping against the harbour. We hauled the lighter seaweed off the drying beach this morning, a place they refer to as the Trokht Boan, the white beach, on account of the rocks just off the foreshore having been bleached over the years to a bright grey and cream. This morning it rained and it made carrying these baskets lashed to our backs more difficult than I had hoped. My back aches here almost all of the time. The rocks and seaweed and rain and surf make for a type of slippiness on the edges of the island, to which, even after almost two years, I'm sure I will never become fully accustomed.

Paulie Óg clinks two sickle-shaped scythes off each other as I approach. I almost expect a spark to appear from them. He's smiling broadly, on the edge of excitement, because a package of comic books an aunt regularly sends to him from America has arrived at the post office in Motebeg. He has a deep interest in these comic books, especially the Superman character, and I think if he were shown how to draw or write one of these comic books that he might enjoy greatly creating a character of his own with strange endowments.

He has shown me often his collection, the absurd narratives in which he has long lost interest. What he seems to intuit now are the developments of the comic strip's style. Paulie Óg, who is a disarmingly intelligent person, seems to be discerning shifts in the look of these things. He often visits my house in the evening and we often have dinner together until it grows dark. He teaches me some rudiments of the Irish language and taught me how to pronounce and spell correctly his name, some place names near to but not on the island and some local surnames. Many months back he brought me the telescope that had been replaced at the schoolhouse, and some evenings we stargaze late into the night awaiting occultations of any kind.

Guinan leaps onto the rear of the boat. It rocks a moment in the dark harbour water. I push a pitchfork into the side of the mound.

I bid farewell to Paulie Óg as I step down onto the boat. It drops some inches as oily water spills in over the lip. The boat bobs and balances as I sit alongside Guinan. We take an oar each and Paulie Óg drops a curl of blue rope onto my lap. I push us off with the tip of my oar and we wobble, then float delicately out into the shining estuary. A swooping gull cries overhead as Guinan circles his oar into the surf and the front tip of the vessel pans left to reveal the white breadth of this body of water. When we are pointing towards the western lighthouse in the distance we know to begin our stroke and reverse towards the mainland. The breeze picks up as we pass the harbour wall, and as we ease along and clear this stone promontory, the island's shoreline reappears, and with it slides into view a giant erratic boulder, covered over in smoke from a throbbing fire begun beneath it over a week ago. Paulie Óg and Jim Guineáon intend tomorrow to split this rock, for reasons so far not wholly clear to me.

'Not a bad day,' says Guinan, as we take another backward stroke and advance further into the estuary.

At Motebeg's harbour the squat and hairy Kriin is waiting at the base of the jetty. His pony and cart are angled up the plane of wet concrete. We ground our gandalow at the lip of the jetty and I leap from it, drag it to a standstill and begin to pile the drier top third of the seaweed into Kriin's cart. Meanwhile, Guinan steps from the boat and loops the length of blue rope through a steel hoop clinking from the barnacle-covered wall. He and Kriin speak for some moments in Irish with shreds of English weaved through, until Kriin produces from behind his back his heavily bandaged hand and the shreds of English grow into sentences that overcome the collapsing strings then atoms of Irish they were speaking.

'You got caught in the end,' says Guinan.

'Still horrid sore. The boy is up in the convent – concussed. They're leaving it all to rot. It's three springs since we last cut and I tried to tell the Tan bastard that he'll ruin the crop.'

This Kriin, who is close to tears, has white hair and thick black eyebrows that remain almost motionless over his otherwise expressive and rubicund face.

'The cutting knife is only good for thatching now,' he concludes.

'Greedy Tan bastard.'

To which Kriin merely nods.

He looks at me transferring the seaweed onto the cart. The pony takes a step backward then one forward. The wheels creak. Two local men in a shallow boat row past. We wave and moments later the inner-estuary water laps against the harbour wall.

Kriin looks to Guinan, 'Every time I pass I can see more of the kelp pushed up onto the rocks. It's covering over the wrack and the whole thing is beginning to smell of piss. I wouldn't pass if I didn't have to ...'

Guinan, who is a patient kind of person, has heard this every fortnight for the last year and yet he shows compassion to this man, and whenever Guinan and I continue on to Kindara he never mentions to me how dull he must find these metronomic complaints. I am unsure if this is because Guinan wouldn't consider it right to or because he wouldn't bother to share with me such an intimate thing as feelings between local folk.

'And how's Nikolas these days?' says Kriin turning to me.

'Very well,' I reply.

'They still treating you like a brother over there?'

'Like a king in exile,' I say.

Kriin and Guinan walk up to the town as I continue lifting the ragged seaweed from our boat to this old and simple cart.

I ask Guinan to check in the post office to see if any letters have arrived and to pick up also my copy of the London *Times*, which I've received here for the last year, though always at least a few days and on occasion as much as a week out of date. Now and then I also purchase the local papers, but each time I hand the paper to Guinan I realize from the excitement and interest with which he reads each article that I am missing most of what is absorbing in this news.

A bell ding-dongs from a distant corner of the town and as the breeze folds over and stretches seaward the quiet but busy rumble of carts, cars and tractors floats from the conurbation out across the harbour and echoes against its walls. I throw the pitchfork back onto the oarweed and dulse mounded upon the vessel, which itself has lifted an inch above the water. I approach Kriin's blinkered and somewhat mangy pony and stroke its blonde flank for a time. I sit up on the quay and wait for Guinan to return.

A brilliant white gannet glides over the expanse of water between the harbour and the far peninsula that cradles the northern side of this town. The gannet's wings slice through an undulating breeze. Some days when I have the time to look at these birds, I think of their bodies as all that is actual of them and their wings as magical extensions lifting and returning the veil of the world, and what I am looking on at is not flight, but suspension between worlds, neither of which I can quite seem to glimpse. The easy flight of a seabird here gives me a sense of satisfaction that outstrips almost any other feelings I have or can expect to have from the world I find myself in now.

I left the Midlands one night soon after the lightning storm, without a word, and went to London to procure a Polish passport. An old university colleague, an Englishman called Smith, came to my aid. For many months I was moved from basement to basement, all dotted through central London, sometimes sharing these rooms with emigrés in similar states of flux. I wonder where those men and women I met have flung themselves off to now. I wonder if they live day to day, like me, tired with fear. Our conversations in these basements in London were kind but guarded – all of us covetous with our plans. It pained me each time I met a fellow Russian traveler that I could not unburden myself or that they could not unburden to me their desires, fears, ends or origins. It angered me to think that such paranoia could take such hold in such dark and seemingly hidden coordinates of the world. I wrote once in this time to Rhatigan saying I would make contact again as soon as I could. Then I returned here in late March of '51. I waited for months before contacting him, and it was some months later before he wrote in return. It was a terse but positive missive. He used my new Polish name, Nikolas Roszak, on the letter as I had asked and he referred to almost nothing of my previous note in which I'd described my time in London and my surreptitious return. He took up our conversation on the technical terms we'd left it, merely telling me that they'd abandoned the secondary benchmark we'd struggled to locate, on account of 'news coming from Dublin that the whole country was to be retriangulated'. He said the old triangulations that had connected Ireland to

Britain through points along the east coast would finally be snipped, thus lifting the country 'in Ordnance-survey terms', he wrote, three metres out of the sea. They'd already begun retriangulating in the North and this work would bring new concrete plinths fitted into hilltops and other vantage points on the land, and from these robust new points, he told me, one could affix one's theodolite, and survey out to unknown points more accurately than before. This retriangulation in the North led up from the Midlands, stemming from a new point on the 'Hill of Ushnagh' and it was from here he, and a team of surveyors, carried out their revised triangulation to a new secondary benchmark sunk deep into a point at the edge of the bog, to an accuracy of an inch and a half over almost thirty miles. 'Accuracy's children have devoured their parents,' he wrote, to which he humorously added that 'Colm and Mel were glad to be off the hook' and he thanked me for my 'contribution'. He finished his neat missive saying if I were ever to pass through again that I should visit to see how the drainage and building works have progressed. Then he signed off, with a P.S. beneath his carefully signed name, claiming that I 'would barely recognize the place'. I imagine him now still surveying parcels of land, trapped between two forces – his aim and the land's indifference, both leading to a point where numbers end and where actual things can begin. And I realize from his memoranda that the industry I had once found so interesting to him was a mere transposing of his guilt and perhaps even his grief for the brother he had killed, as if the suppression of these feelings beneath the machinery of his industry could somehow cauterize him from the pain. I wonder often if this method has brought him success.

In my most recent reply I told him that I'd written many months before to French, but that I had not received a letter in return. I am certain French is not illiterate, though I know people can hide such perceived lack with genius, but, with his not responding, I was concerned that I had either offended him or that he did not trust me. Then, on certain nights in the quiet of my gatehouse I'd wake and stare at the underside of the roof listening for the approach of boots on stone, hating myself for transforming this good French into a dangerous loose end. Then after a while I began to worry less and forgot almost completely about him until one day it occurred to me to ask the islanders here about his brother, but they said that they had not ever heard of this man, French, from the Midlands.

By the time Guinan and I land at Kindara the sun has come and gone at least a dozen times. One of the plant workers stands at the top of the jetty. He is skinny. His mass of dark hair makes his head seem out of proportion to his body, as if his head could at any moment topple off. He is releasing down into the water a flat steel-framed trailer. Beyond the tip of the ramp stalls a tractor, coughing puffs of blue smoke skyward. I step down into the water and lead the gandalow, in bumps, onto the frame. I stumble on the fronds of seaweed gathering at my feet. I right myself and feel the weight of the gandalow fall away as it meets the frame beneath, and the whole thing rises and steadies. The young man lashes the chain at the end of the rope to the tractor, clambers in and puts the tractor into a low clattering gear from which the engine of the machine erupts and strains. So loud and noisy and smoky is this old tractor that one might think it was wrenching all of the seaweed in the estuary up onto dry land. Guinan walks after the load as I step out of the water sloshing against the rocks. He disappears towards the low-lying industrial buildings in the mid-distance, to inspect the weight to which this load amounts.

A plane appears in the sky towards the west. It draws out a descent on the airstrip near the village of Shrool. It's a small aircraft and its propellors thrum in a way I would describe almost as welcoming. I imagine the pilot rattling around up there, looking down upon the western side of the island, taking in the old church called Saint Enda's, protruding from the side of the westernmost hill, ten minutes from my gatehouse. Around this church are dotted headstones with the name Guinane, and the other variations thereof, carved into their faces. I've spent many hours walking around these headstones noting the family names and how they zigzag back into the distant past. These people don't seem to mind the doomed monotony of their family patterns appearing and disappearing on the surface of this island.

Since I've been here, the sea and the currents and the quiet have returned me to some of the mathematics I studied after I left Kazan with Rogkov. At first, in the evenings, to dispel my fears of the dark and of the entities that might emerge from it and drag me back in, I decided to revisit the most basic of number elements, to see what light might still lie in them. I tried to approach what is visual and tactile in numbers because I've come to realize that the emphasis, while I was in university in Moscow and London, was to think of numbers mostly through the processes of algebra. And I realize a more visual approach would have suited my sensibility, and as I come to terms with this here, my sense of guilt at my lack of mathematical endowment crumbles too. In the candle- and lamplight of my gatehouse I count out rational numbers at their most fundamental. I push my meagre pieces of furniture to one side and place in a line on the floor four stones of medium size, each a foot apart: 1, 2, 3, 4. Then between each number I place a sea-shell to denote one of the innumerable fractions between each whole. To the left of the first stone I open out a line of yellow rope perpendicular to the line of medium-sized stones, and with this I designate the point of zero. Then, I place four further medium-sized stones to the left of the length of rope to create the negative numbers -1, -2, -3 and -4 and between these negative numbers I denote, with more of these delicate seashells, negative fractions. I take then a tiny sea-smoothed pebble and I hold it, between my fingers, a foot above the first stone to the right of the rope. I don't consider this pebble hovering above its number as an object in space, but as a phantasm-function of the whole number below. In university I could put numbers through any variety of algebraic functions and differential equations and arrive often at the correct, and methodically correct, answer, but I never understood until these recent evenings in my gatehouse what the imaginary part of a number really was, the part that hovers above the rational whole number, guiding it from the dimensions of flatness into the next dimension of curves, and by doing this I have begun to see more clearly the form, meaning and potential of the complex number: $1+1i$. After this I came to realize too that it is this kind of number that allows me to now see how a straight line, if looked at in a certain way, can also be the shadow cast by a curved line, and if a projected curve can be also a straight line then the direction in which other possible parallel lines extend too, towards the infinite, can be imagined, and in this space between the infinite and the finite emerge countless other possible parallel lines that might be the shadows of shadows of intersecting curves from other places and other times, cast by entities with other desires and ends.

While playing with these rocks, shells and ropes, a strange recalibration then occurred within me – rising from the crumbling sense of shame, a sense of self-worth began to gather, and I have permitted this regathering to give me confidence, even though none of what I have relearned will ever be of use to me or ever need to be displayed. But at least I've come to realize that geometric visualizations without their mirroring algebra flail in the realm of application, and I realize also that the satisfying thread drawings and visualizations of my youth were curious but ultimately useless shapes dangling wantonly in the groundless air.

In the last number of months, at the end of a full day with these islanders, when I sit in the second room I've constructed within my gatehouse, I think about the gaps in the language I encounter here. These people often blend Irish with English, and from the core of this emerges sentence structures that belong, I think, to neither. The gaps I encounter in this syntax often now remind me of my late teenage years when I first began, with a feverish earnestness, to learn English, and with these new word gaps I've begun to see at last clearly the sickly Bishop Pyotr from Chekhov's tale 'The Bishop', and how his nature in this story is shown only by the responses of those around him: his parishioners; his niece; his mother, Marya; and his colleague Father Sisoy. And I apply the connective tissue between these people who surround Bishop Pyotr to the sentences I misunderstand here on the island, and instead of asking the islanders to fill in the gap, by explaining the word I do not understand, I instead play a game with myself where the word I do not understand becomes, to me: the 'Chekhov's Bishop' of the sentence. And I imagine the meaning of the word I do not understand by how the words around it behave in its presence, and I then picture the mystery word as a hole, with me standing in its base, awaiting the facial expressions of the other words as they gather around the hole, wondering as to what the incomprehensible whimper emanating from it might be or mean. The problem, when I first studied mathematics, was that I perceived the disconnect between what I could see in geometrics and what I could not see in its distant algebraic form as a blind spot, a deficiency, and it is this sense of lack that eroded slowly through my person. And it was not until recently in my gatehouse on this island, when these blind spots became instead perspective-giving holes, that I realized that this revised approach had also pointed me towards this new way of viewing numbers as elemental things like stones, shells, ropes and pebbles being carefully manipulated in the dark.

Guinan and I are followed by three dolphins all of the way back across the estuary. They emerge, shine, dip and descend into the water as we go. They circle us many times, mocking the turgidity with which we proceed. Guinan told me that he found a dolphin's spine on the beach one day and that it was the most beautiful thing he'd ever seen. He said he considered taking it as a decoration for above the hearth in his cottage, as a white crown for the licking flames beneath – but then, he said, without a further thought he cast this 'interlocking wave of calcium' back into the water, because he couldn't imagine such a thing being anywhere other than in the sea, where at least it can continue, he claimed, to move or to rest in a place where gravity makes itself less acutely known.

GENEALOGICAL CHART of the ISLAND
from cemetery headstones in Saint Enda's Church

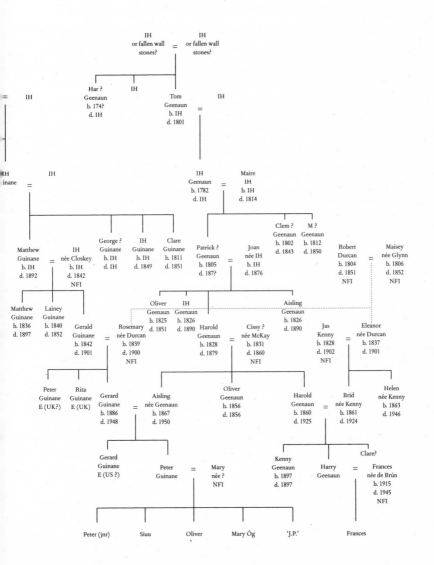

NFI: Not From (not born on) the Island
IH: Indecipherable Headstone
E (UK): Emigrated to United Kingdom?
E (US): Emigrated to United States?

I bid farewell to Guinan at the harbour and walk up the hill, past the well and to Guineáon's home. I'm harvesting kelp with this family later this afternoon, when the tide comes back in. Guineáon might be considered the least successful of all the farmers on this island. He drinks the most too, but he is an affable drunk and falls asleep often, in a sudden slump, his mass of red hair cascading over his broad wind-worn face.

Hens and chickens scatter from his door as I enter his cottage. The family are around the table – two lamps glowing at either end. A cylindrical wicker basket of oranges lies on its side in the middle of the table. Some oranges have tumbled out across the timber surface, which is so worn it shines. Oranges and bananas and such exotic things appear often on this island and I have to guess if these things have been washed up onto the shore, or if there is some shop or market on the mainland where they can be purchased and about which I have yet to be told. Sometimes, though, I imagine smugglers' boats from northern Africa or Spain or Portugal landing silently here at night and dispensing small fractions of their goods to these eager and well-connected islanders.

The house is sultry. An open fire throbs to my left sending smoke up into the chimney, which thuds from time to time with the passing sea wind. Jim Guineáon sits at the head of the table peeling oranges and casting the skins onto the floor beside him. A tang of citrus mixes with the smoke. Jim's wife, Rose, a slim person with long greying hair, who tolerates me only as a worker, pips each orange as Jim hands them to her. It is a young family and the youngest, a slight and blonde girl, Anna, is at the end of the table thumping the slicer's blade over and back as the next eldest, a small and partly lame boy, John, his hair as red as his father's, pushes the segments of orange through, wincing as he goes. On the other side of the slicer stands the next eldest, the family's favourite, a dark-haired girl called Rosemary. She catches the slices in a bright blue tub, which she hands to the eldest, James, a tall and pensive adolescent, stationed at the oven. He then takes a marmalade jar out and fills it with these orange slices, pours hot sugared water in, pushes a misbehaving mass of his auburn hair from his face, then caps the jar with a circle of patterned greaseproof paper and slips an elastic band around the rim. He places the jar onto the table beside the window, where the sunlight falls and glistens upon the dozen or so receptacles of warm marmalade.

'God bless us and preserve us!' calls Jim.

'The family Guineáon,' I reply, as I close the door and step towards the kitchen basin to pour water over my hands. I look out the window and see the wind has strengthened again. A large sycamore tree beside the second basalt erratic of the island bends. Though it stands in the field behind Guineáon's house, the field is the property of Guinane. The young leaves and branches of this sycamore shake inharmoniously.

'You'll have a drop of tea?'

'Yes, please,' I say.

An hour later and we are all at the westerly shore. The Trokht Boan is almost completely clear of the out-rushing tide. The family Guineáon unfurl a large ball of rope, which they refer to as 'the ceekjayn'. It is a length of intertwined braids of straw into which they now, along its length, twist shreds of seaweed. They don't invite me to take part in these intricate tasks, as if by keeping me at arm's length from such things they will protect, from outsiders such as me, the finer secrets of their trades. While they weave their rope, I walk from clump to clump of seaweed, grasp the frond and with my sickle slice. This sort of egg wrack, they tell me, should be cut halfway down its stem. They warn me if I touch the holdfast, the root, at the base of the organism that the plant will be ruined. After almost two years here – and despite my work being judged by them always as satisfactory – they still advise me so.

I stand and peer out at the sea. My hair blows around, throwing itself upon my brow. The lenses in my spectacles have filled over again in mist. I clean them and put them back on. The heaving sea is entering that moment of suspension between when the tide stops going out and when it begins coming in. I bend once more, and grasp and hack and bend and grasp and cut again, and then I cast a slithering handful aside. Last month, at a strangely low tide, we'd stepped further out into the foreshore and took in a mixed harvest of nori, karikiin and great clumps of the fibrous sea spaghetti. The tide at this time of year shifts with incredible speed. Until I arrived here, I always thought of tides as slow things.

Jim approaches and while addressing us all he points to the rock line at the base of the Trokht Boan, 'We've another hour to cut, then we'll draw in what we have. It'll be enough!'

Jim's two sons, one tall one tiny, string out, from both arms of the inlet, their length of seaweed rope. It floats on the water in a ragged loop. These two boys then stumble on the rocks as they fasten the ends of the rope back to the shore.

In from the waves come the rest of the Guineáons, pulling their knives and sickles as they bend, grasp and cut. While I work like this, the differences between the families on this island become most apparent to me. The Guinans often stop and straighten to talk to each other, for a time, in drifts of Irish and English most usually about the recent matches of football and hurling on the mainland. Paulie Óg, who is as pleasant to his parents and his young sister, Eta, as he is interesting and pleasant to me, chatters away into the gurgles and the splashing water. I can tell his parents are as proud of his natural erudition as of his energy while he works, though I can tell also that they wonder about where all of this will lead and why he has no interest in leaving the island. More recently he speaks about this large erratic boulder down at the shore that he and Guineáon are aiming to split, and to this his family has always fallen silent.

The quiet Guinanes, on the other hand, all with the darkest of eyes I've ever seen, barely utter a word to each other, solemnly cutting and throwing handfuls of weed, systematically working their way across their patch in a line, with me appendaged at one end. Then, when they wander or cycle back to their house, their crop safely netted down on the higher end of the shore, they begin to talk once more. They are the most subdued of the four families and I always assumed this was because their family saw most death on this island, but while inspecting the headstones in the grave-yard, to the rear of the church, I noted that the dead of their family, or at least the story of death in their family, is a largely natural and happy one, as it were, and I realized that the solemnity that engulfs this family must come from the sense that they feel they are edging closer, almost in a statis-tical sense, to a great family sadness and that their quietness with each other is an unspoken preparation for the painful first absence all but one of them will feel.

The Geenauns, then, have the smallest sliver of fore-shore and prefer to be considered progressive dairy farmers. They own a bull, a small number of limousine cattle and over twenty calves. I often see Harry Geenaun and his young daughter, Frances, who must only be eight or so, take their boat back to the livestock mart in Motebeg each Thursday. Geenaun inherited his improvised boat from his father: four galvanized gates in a square, afloat on the estuary with sometimes up to ten cattle stomping, in great fear, around their tilting cage. Geenaun's wife passed away during childbirth and, on the few occasions I help them with a crop of seaweed, they seem to work as if they are on a brief holiday from their grief or perhaps they are merely glad to be away from the more serious business of their dairy and meat farming. I find labouring with them to be at once peaceful and alienating; their pleasure for the work exists in a place asymptotic to me.

'In she comes,' cries Rose, standing, a leg either side of a rock draped over in ink-green seaweed. The waves crash up and into the inlet. The water and foam rushes then gathers beautifully amid the rocks before it pools away. When one looks closely, the chaos in the smallest square inch of this place becomes dizzying in its plummeting curvatures. Here is a wetland mapped out with a constantly collapsing Cartesianism of intensities and it seems to me that all who live here grasp this without a need to elucidate it. It seems to me that the grammar of behaviour here, that meets this aspect of the place most naturally, is a grammar of perpetual falling, and I have come to understand that it is moments like these that French was perhaps referring to when he spoke about the language of this place – the language that so entranced his brother, a language built off this elusive and crumbling grammar.

We bend and stand and bend and cut for another number of minutes. I can hear the two girls are giddy at the thought of this bending and cutting coming at last to an end. They, like me, still find the tide coming in exceptional.

Jim and his eldest boy, James, this lanky youth, walk outwards along the left and right arms of the inlet. The rest of us step back up the shore to the shingle. The waves approach and the wind whips again as the sun sears through the edge of a breaking cloud. I am suddenly at once hot and somewhat cold. The tide rises and as it encroaches and fills the inlet, the sea wrack we've cut free of the rocks rises too in a dark haggard miasma of minerals. As the inlet floods, Jim and James heave on the ends of their line of ceekjayn. The mound grows as the ceekjayn gathers the floating seaweed in. The two pull harder until it all heaps together in the crashing tumbling water. Both of them begin to walk backwards along the craggy arms of the inlet, hauling the mound in inches towards the shore. The waves break under, over and upon the island of seaweed, now toppling then resting on the shingle. Gulls circle, calling overhead. John, this limping but determined young boy, wheels a barrow to the heap that is now sitting and slipping upon itself. It presents to us a type of formless, frictionless inertia. A crab appears from a crease in the base and little Anna chases it away, her fingers like pincers hovering over the back of this orange creature. An eel slithers up and out and behind. Some fish flap wretchedly around until Rosemary steps forward, squats, pushes her dark hair from her face, flips the fish onto the sand and then drops them into a metal bucket where I can hear them squirm, gasp and thump. I approach the mound, brandishing my pitchfork, and silently load the wheelbarrow. The seaweed crunches up the handle as I force the prongs of the implement in and twist. From the neighbouring inlet Jim has pushed his gandalow out into the sea. He floats around just clear of the peninsula. The wind whips up again and the sky darkens, while white birds swerve in rampant arcs beyond him. The water is deepening, but he can still reach the base of the channel with his stave. He stands there, bobbing about, beyond the tip of the small rocky tongue of land. The distant horizon line meets him at his waist. Another gust whips in. I almost expect Jim to break into song. Instead I see my father as a young man singing across the bog to my approaching mother, as my brother and I straighten from our lifting and cutting. She has her arms outstretched and is smiling, the breeze whipping her yellow hair across and obscuring her face. She wears her sky-blue apron, and from the pockets she pulls, as she steps towards us – white clouds skudding across the plains behind – some cuts of meat and three apples.

'Get a barrow of the good stuff out here to me, lads!' calls Jim, as the brown Kazani land around him falls away into heaving waves of lilac.

I drop my pitchfork and grasp the leading end of the barrow, now full of sea spaghetti, and with John we stumble out onto the rocks to the right of the inlet. This is where the pain in my brittle Russian back stems from – slipping and adjusting and falling and righting my way across these rocks with my hands behind my back, directed and shooed and shushed by the eldest or some days the second-eldest or some days the third-eldest of the island's sons. We reach the end of the tiny peninsula and draw level with the vessel and we tip the contents of the barrow over the gunwale. Then we return and return again, over and back across this inde-cipherable ground until Jim, from his tilting boat, utters at last, 'That'll do.'

Before I leave Guineáon's cottage that night, Rose comes to the door and hands me three filleted fish wrapped up in paper and, with this, an orange and a plum. I thank her as I pull on my jacket and bid her and the rest of the family good evening. I walk back to the well, where I retrieve my bag and take a bucket of water and my carbide-battery lamp. As I crest the hill back to my gatehouse I sense clouds rushing past overhead. The water in my pail below sloshes over the rim and onto the road. I shine the lamp ahead, then into a field where I spy in conclave three white hares and one grey. I can hear the distant astonished breath of the sea. The high hedges gather either side of me as I descend the hill and with it comes the smell of soil, and for a moment this encroachment transports me to the landscapes that drop and rise around Rhatigan's home in the centre of the mainland. When I arrive at my gatehouse I turn on my lamps, begin a small fire and fry up my fillets of plaice, with every intention, in the quiet of the late evening, of opening my letters and reading my newspaper. But after I eat, I slump asleep on my chair and only rouse again in the darkness, cursing the dead lamp and the wasted paraffin. Then, I put myself to bed, hoping the animals outside, or the seagulls above me, or the sunlight itself will wake me at a useful hour in the morning.

2

There is a small island that lies half of a mile to the north-west of the sliver of beach at the foot of my hill. They call this tiny land mass Ilon ier Mjor – island of the big man.

The ink-blue dark of early morning is lifting around me, as the choppy estuary water slaps the flanks of my boat. A cool breeze passes across my face and my knuckles. The day is just on the other side of dawn. The dark is rising skyward now, revealing a horizontal band of light in the distance, as if the horizon, once reorganized through the lens of my spectacles, is about to begin bleeding in opening strands across my retina. I turn and begin to make out the contours of the small island as it emerges out of the sea.

The difference in the soil between this island and the larger one from which I come is great. On the larger island the topsoil consists of a foot of sand, then stone, clay, then sand. This tiny island has soil so dense and fertile that it feels like it has been transported from the richest of tillage farms.

It seems somewhat a shame that the soil type from one island cannot be transplanted with the soil type of the other. The smaller land mass, though only an acre or thereabouts, is covered in hedges, scrub, grass and hillocks and has three fine leaning sycamore trees on the leeward side all growing a dozen yards or so from the freshwater stream that trickles and meanders across the island and into the sea.

Every Saturday morning I either row over to the island and go ashore, or I stay in my boat and circle the island to see if the dog that was put here by Jim Guineáon, over a year ago, is still alive. She is a black border collie and Jim had put her there because she was designated as wicked. She had smuggled herself onto our island – leaping one day onto the front of Jim's boat at Motebeg quay. He didn't notice her until she leapt off again at the harbour on the island. The four families first discussed shooting her, then they discussed bringing her back to Motebeg, but Jim, who felt responsible for this trouble also felt trapped between two types of guilt: he himself could not kill the dog nor condone having it killed for him, and he couldn't unleash her back into Motebeg where her behaviour would almost certainly have led to her being put down.

'There's nothing inherently wrong with a dog being wicked,' he said.

The dog had fallen into the habit of sleeping under the front porch of the schoolhouse, so early one morning he took out a sheep hook, snuck up and snared the dog around the neck. He led it wriggling and whining to the harbour, where he boated the barking animal across to this island and there he left her. The island hosts rabbits and otters and birds, and if the dog was clever and limber enough it would survive, he reckoned. So Jim turned from the island that morning and has not returned since, and I always thought he had put the creature out of his mind until six months later when he – having somehow learned that I made these weekly trips over to see this hound – asked me quietly one early afternoon: 'Is the little bitch still alive?'

When I told him that she was, he muttered, more so to himself than to me, and with a clenching fist forming in his right hand, 'Good girl. Good girl yourself.'

There's a tiny shingle beach on the sheltered side of the island, and it is at this beach I land. The hull of the boat lifts, then grinds across the surface. The dog, who I've begun calling Lupita, appears from over a rock and does what she does every time I arrive: she stands still for almost a minute, her nose up, smelling the air, then she paces and barks and howls for almost another. In the last three months, in her barks and yowls I'm beginning to read expressions of great joy, but I can never be wholly sure. My family had no use for a dog while I was growing up, and I did not have society with people who used one either, so when I step onto her beach I still do so with hesitation. Some days, so unsure am I of her mood that I often retreat from the beach, leave a few patted balls of fat or leftover food, and row back across the broad channel between these two nodes of land.

She bounds down the beach towards me and stops all of a sudden, her ears upright and her dark eyes darting around my outline, and she barks once more. Then she drops to the ground and I can tell by the tremor in her tail that she is in a good mood and will receive me well. I step from the boat and onto the beach and reach my curled fingers out to her. She sniffs for a moment or two then, with her tail beating from side to side, she begins to lick my hand, the knuckles, the fingers, the back, the palm, until I feel like I can reach over her head and rub her neck, by which time she has curled herself towards me and is leaning her warmth into my shin. Of late I come here and relay to her what is happening in the world and how I feel, and how crimson the blood from my anus has become, and often, if the weather is clement, we sit for a while on the beach and I say very little until I leave. I do not set foot on any other part of her island, as if what she does there is for her alone, but I am sure those parts are littered with the bones of savaged young rabbits, waterfowl and otters. On quiet and darker days I tell her how much I miss my dear Matvei and how, since the shock of his death, I seem to have marooned myself into a sexual exile, a sort of numbness, and I tell her, though I cannot make sense of the comfort I take from this numbness, that I do know while I remain marooned from myself like this there is at least a good chance I will remain untouched.

I think about the time when Matvei was killed eight years ago, on a train from Moscow to Leningrad. He was at last back working again, this time on a screenplay for his friend Pudovkin, a seasoned filmmaker. It would have been Matvei's and my first meeting since the war, and we had, with great excitement, arranged to meet that evening at Moscow station in Leningrad, but what I met instead was his covered-over corpse being carried from the train with policemen and a doctor in tow. The white sheet shrouding his body had one red circle slowly enlarging through the fabric. They would not let me see the body. I wrote to his mother, Yelena, days later, promising that I would find out how he died. But my queries, tearful and desperate as they were, were met with hostile then increasingly suspicious rebuttals. I realize, looking down at Lupita wriggling against my legs, that I would happily remain in this state of numbed fear for every remaining day of my life, if I knew that at the end of it all I could once more see Matvei, stepping from that train and greeting me in his arms.

I pull my rowboat further up onto the beach and take a seat on a rock, inhale a fingernail of snuff and begin to smoke a cigarette. The wind whistles across the modest dunes, waving the grass around on top. Lupita jumps into the boat and looks back out at me, then sniffs vigorously around its extents. She is still young. She springs from the boat then steps up alongside me sniffing my boots, legs, the orange in my coat pocket, and I tell her about what I read in the newspaper by candlelight this morning; I tell her I have learned that Stalin has died. I tell her also that my old colleague Malenkov is taking control and that I never thought I would see the day when our dear leader would die – I never thought, I tell her, rubbing her belly, that I would see the day I could consider returning home.

She sniffs my cigarette and I tip from the top a growing bend of ash. A gust thuds overhead, shivering out lines of yellow and green. The waves lap upon the stones and grey-lemon shingle. I tell her that I do not know, though, if I have the stomach to return.

I go to my boat and lift out my bag. Wrapped up within is one of the fillets of plaice Rose gave to me the night before. It's fried but has cooled hard. I lay it out on the ground. Lupita gallops forward and eats it in three shuddering gulps. Then she licks the paper until it lifts, turns and drifts away. She chases the paper down the small beach, but with the next gust it is picked up and onto the water. She watches this square of white paper float there for almost a minute, whining through her nose. Then she retreats a few steps and jumps forward, barking, and I wonder where on this island she goes to when she is afraid. She returns to me and sniffs at my feet. Before I clamber back onto my rowboat to return to my island, I bend and take Lupita's dark and beautiful head into my hands, and I tell her that she is a good girl.

Back on the island, in my crackling gatehouse home, I stand by the window, and in the morning light I reread *The Times* making clear to myself that this news of Stalin is not some hoax or that something is not terribly incorrect. I read and reread the pages about his death and burial and successor over and again as if I am searching for some code beneath the newsprint that will tell me to stay away. I picture my tiny old apartment in Leningrad, not three streets from the offices of the State Geometers. I imagine it still empty, with dust all over my papers, my books, photographs of my family, my clothes. I imagine the letters and newspapers mounded up against the inside of the front door, and I picture the drab view out of my apartment window onto the gable of the school building opposite. Then I imagine all of this ripped apart and overturned and rifled through by strangers. I try to see myself piecing this disturbance back together.

I turn to my rickety table beside the open fire, take out a sheet of paper and begin a letter to Malenkov congratulating him on his ascent. I see the amused expression he wore on his face that day when he first learned of how I had, during my time in England, 'wasted the people's money'. It was during an interview for a position at the Special Committee for Rocket Technology when we were discussing the tracing of ballistics through the air. Malenkov, a portly, dark-haired and buttoned-up man, could tell, despite my name and its pedigree, that I had neither the intuition nor ingenuity to be a true avant-garde of his group. When he began discussing the most rudimentary developments in codebreaking, random numbers and closed-loop systems, and when I was unable to answer any of his most simple technical queries, his round and up till then chummy face fell, and rushing in behind, with a frightening speed, coursed his natural malevolence. Malenkov, for such a committed Party man, had a pragmatic attitude towards recruitment – he took on the best-educated and most-talented of engineers and mathematicians to lead his increasingly professionalized departments, instead of those thinkers most aligned with the dominant dialectical ideals. But he obviously had his limits, and I had angered him. When we returned to this idea of measuring anticipated positions of targets in the sea or in the air, I, trying to save face and to show him I had learned something from my time in university in London, pulled before us a piece of paper and drew onto it a single upward arc, and at the end of this arc of regular curvature I dropped a vertical dotted line. I framed a length of this arc to the left of the dotted line with my finger and thumb and turned to Malenkov's briefly reanimated face, and said, 'If we can take this piece of the past and extend it beyond the dotted line of the present we will be able to predict to good accuracy a moment in the future; and if we can compute the future, Comrade Malenkov, even the smallest pico-second of it, then we can aim and control the fate of whatever will arrive there.'

To this Malenkov, having developed a macabre obsession with the controlling of the future, responded: 'Excellent.'

But I crumpled up the piece of paper I'd been drawing on, and pushed it to one side, saying to this thug, 'It is, but I do not think, anymore, that it is right.'

'Lobachevsky,' he replied, retrieving his pen from my hand.

I looked up at Malenkov, but he only continued to smile. I wondered how many people he had killed soon after smiling at them in this way.

'It is not right, because it's a future that can only be won with computing horsepower,' I continued, 'it is a type of future that doesn't belong in the realm of good people.'

'The realm of good people,' he replied, this time his smile radiant, 'that is a good one, comrade,' and he began to laugh.

I turn back to my table, lift my pen and after a few obsequious lines of greeting I fold the paper up, throw it onto the ashes in my dying fire and leave for Saturday morning service in the church.

As I walk up the winding island road I hear the bell of Saint Enda's church in the near distance ring. The bell is far larger than a church of this size needs. It sounds often as if it proclaims its devotion not out to the sea but back towards the mainland from where it, I'm told, arrived. The children here take turns ringing the bell in its tower; then, these children, flushed, return to act at the mass service as altar boys and on rare occasions altar girls. The priest, a Father Dahjerti, who comes from the mainland every Saturday and Sunday morning to administer the liturgy, is a tall and elegant man. I imagine if he were not a priest he would be married and would by now have sired many fine children. His services are brief and his homilies light. I picture him now lifting sacred objects from the safe in the sacristy and preparing these gleaming chalices and plates for the holy hour.

As I arrive at the gate to the church, the sun returns between two enormous cumulonimbus, and the trees around the edifice throw waving shadows upon its worn rubble walls.

I've told the islanders here that I am Polish, and that I fought and was imprisoned in the war and, after my release, instead of rebuilding a life in Poland I escaped to pilgrimage to the most holy of Catholic lands and on those lands to the most remote or peaceful of places. I tell them I've turned to God.

Looking on at this church, imagining these good islanders quietly taking their seats within, I decide that I cannot attend this service, so I turn back down the roadway and walk past my gatehouse and towards the sea. I arrive at the narrow strand at the base of the hill, from where, if I go east along the rocks, I can circumnavigate the island in no more than an hour. I have done this clockwise and anticlockwise often.

I stumble over loose rocks, slippery with seaweed, and continue into the shadows of forty yards of limestone cliff. Out of the yawning chasm opening out from this pit of Stalin's demise comes to me at last an image of my mother – her face, when I was a young boy. She is sitting at the end of my bed reading to my dozing younger brother, Evgenii, and me the playful adventures of the misbehaving German boys Max and Moritz. She is reading to us with humour the quiet brutality of these youths. I can see her broad face, her dark eyebrows, her soft features now slowed down like a film playing to an audience in an auditorium of which I am no longer part. I have not allowed her face to form in my mind since I have come to this island. It seemed to me that if I could not stand in the land of her blue eyes, her wide mouth, her dimpled cheeks, then it would be an insult for me to even try to visualize her. But today it is at least possible to imagine returning to that land where I might stand again, in a breeze, and think clearly of my mother's face – framed in her loose wavering curls of fair hair – and let it fill my vision.

During the quieter evenings, when I first arrived here on this island, I would only permit myself to imagine my mother's face when she was a young girl – a figure I have not ever seen in person. I would arrange at either end of the table in my gatehouse two candles, then take a seat at one end of the table and look at these flickering flames – one in the near ground and one in the mid-ground. I would remove my spectacles and flick sufficient snuff into my eyes to make them water and through these tears the mid-ground candle would come into focus and the candle nearest to me would fall into softness and, as this mid-ground candle danced in a draughtless night, I would imagine the flame as a near-ground candle to my mother, as this child, positioned at the other end of my table studying a lurid flame belly-dancing there before her, but long ago, when she was still with the full faculty of sight, sitting at a kitchen table, a continent and a half away, moments before she stood to leave for bed to sleep in a room similarly dark to the one I would sit in in my gatehouse – but hers in a small apartment in the lower floor of a newly built block of three- and four-storey buildings on the outskirts of her hometown of Kazan.

From this arrangement of candles and darkness I would wonder as to the origins of this serious young girl's face forming before me in the light, but after a while it became clear to me that I was merely reconstructing its features from those of my sister, Varvara – a person I have grown to hate despite her face being so close to my mother's in appearance.

The temperature drops. A cold wind switches in across the sea. I lean back against the craggy wall of the cliff. From the rough vertical stone grow outcrops of grass and lichens. They appear as adamant citadels, hundreds of them, protruding up and out along the canting plane of rock. From the grass-fringed ridge out swoop three seagulls, a gannet with its black-edged wings spread wide and two tiny white-bellied plovers. They veer into the breeze, wobble, swoop back and disappear. The cliff slopes downward to a ragged finger of limestone that peaks and troughs and peaks and rumbles into the sea where the waves run, press and foam. I climb up to this black shard of stone as the waves beat after me. My trousers are now wet and I can feel the water soaking my foot clothes and my shoes. I drag my legs from the sea and heave myself onto the crags, where I stumble and slip a moment, before finding footing on an edge of shale – from which I push and jump onto the flagstones beyond.

The foreshore opens up. This handsome length of strand is where the islanders come most often to bathe. The beach falls off steeply into the water, but the currents of the sea there are gentle and predictable. One afternoon in late May after I first arrived here, I was lying on the sand, sunbathing. My eyes were closed as I listened to the water, the wind and the birds. Someone approached. It was the teacher from the schoolhouse beside the well on the hill. She, in a light-blue cotton dress, was carrying in her right hand her leather shoes and the sun was breaking across her blonde curls, the wind pushing them against the side of her face. She was, in that moment, what might be referred to as fair. She sat down beside me and introduced herself as Ellen.

'Nikolas,' I replied.

I put out my hand and she took it. She looked over my chest and legs, lingering for a moment at the knot of bone where my once-snapped shin had poorly set, and read that I was not ashamed at her seeing me like this.

'You must be this Polish visitor, so.'

I nodded and smiled.

'They tell me you are pilgrimaging,' she said. 'Where were you before you landed here?'

I told her I was near the centre of the country for almost two months.

'Klonmiknoijjsz, then,' she said, to which I nodded.

I could tell she didn't believe what I was claiming.

'You teach,' I said, 'at the school. How long have you been teaching there?'

'Three years,' she replied in a sing-song voice. 'It was supposed to be a six-month substitution, but the teacher before me fell ill and couldn't bear returning. He was old and decided to retire a few years earlier than expected. He was well liked here too, you know,' she said, rubbing her shoulders and peering out at the sea. Then she returned her gaze to me. 'He'd taught the parents and their sisters and brothers.

And I was told that when he began teaching here there were a hundred people. The families were distraught when they heard news of his retirement, though,' she said, and she picked up a handful of sand and threw it over my knuckles.

She spoke like someone in their early twenties, but she must have been over forty. There was grey mingling with the blonde at her temples and the most delicate of crow's feet were forming at the sides of her eyes, but they seemed longer than normal, and when she smiled they suddenly became severe.

'They made a big deal of his going,' she continued, as she eased the rising flap of her dress back down over her calves and ankles.

She was sitting in that cross-kneed way that women in dresses sit when they recline on a beach, one outstretched arm elegantly behind. I guessed she had seen such a pose in a Hollywood film of some kind, or a poster for a Hollywood film, until she twisted away from me, thrust her legs out before her and leaned back onto her elbows and suddenly she resembled an old Irish man sitting with his back to a bar in a hostelry, about to issue a witticism. I spied a holy medal resting between a fold in her brassiere and her skin, and above the holy medal a freckle with another smaller freckle alongside. She pushed some strands of her waving hair back out of her face, and I could feel that she was making apparent, by her simply sitting there, our suitability in age and circumstance. A breeze blew up the beach. I reached out to gather up my trousers and pull them on and I took my foot clothes out of my shoes and put them on also. I lifted my shirt from the sand and shook it out. She remained sitting in that inelegant way, looking out over the water and sometimes squinting, like a farmboy, up at me. She said nothing until I lay back down beside her. Some sand had landed on her cheek and I realized that her cheeks were wet. I assumed it was the dust and the breeze watering her eyes.

She stood and picked up her shoes.

'I'm walking back to the harbour,' she said.

'Very well,' I replied.

There is no one bathing here today. A white triangle of plastic has become stuck in the middle of the beach between a jagged stone and a chunk of dried-out driftwood. The shred of plastic flutters in a noisy zzZZZzzzz. The dunes of this beach rise gently to the right, then turn and fall to what might be called the beginnings of pasture, which gather up to a luscious hill and a natural dip, and it is in there, no more than a linear half-mile away, that the islanders all now sit on benches, or stand, or kneel on the slabbed-out floor of the church, as the Latin liturgy proceeds and the morphing clouds pass by overhead. The church was built for a much larger community, and even though at each service all of the families of the island attend in full, the place always seems to me quite empty. The families sit at the frontmost pews either side of the altar, praying, while I look on at them from my usual seat down at the narrow nave entrance. To the rear of the altar always glows an ancient stained-glass window held in place with pointed-fifth arcs of cut stone, and it is to this Fr Dahjerti turns during each mass and exhorts phrase after phrase of Latin to which the families before me respond in monotonal thrums. When I churched in Kazan it felt like we were addressing the skies; here it seems as if they are addressing the earth.

A young man in a small boat putters out from behind an arm of the mainland – it is the lighthouse keeper on his way to the outer peninsula to check on his lamps and equipment. On foggy nights a faint glow can be seen beyond the headland, but the sweeping shaft of light from the house never reaches up into the estuary itself. A cloud passes overhead leaving behind it drifts of rain. Some days here it can at any moment at once rain and not rain. This young lighthouse keeper looks over to me and, plunging seaward, waves. I signal back as he disappears around the shore. I pull my orange from my pocket and peel the skin off in one tattered piece. I throw the peel onto the beach where it is picked up by a tame incoming wave and I watch the opening orange land mass, this continent from another planet in another galaxy, float off upon the lilting water. I push a quarter of this orange into my mouth, and continue along the shore, as an acid sweetness drenches the back of my throat.

While I round the strand on the north-western edge of the island, the distant tower bell begins its wind-warped tinkle. I imagine one of the children being carried up and down in the dark, clinging desperately to the bell rope as the families wander in the sun outside, along the hill, away from this somewhat industrialized holy hour, of two, in their week. Another cloud passes overhead as I spy Paulie Óg walking across the shore before me. His head of brown curls is down and his fingers are to his eyes. Saturday service seems to always alter him and to make him thoughtful, impermeable, until the next time I see him, a day or two after these mass services, and he has regained his openness and former spirits. Behind him plumes the huge smoking rock. It stands some yards landward of the high-tide shoreline. Jim Guineáon suggested last year they attempt at last to split this object. It was then merely a loose proposal, but it was seized upon by Paulie Óg. Jim brought me to the rock a few weeks ago and showed me where one of his ancestors had tried before to break it open. In a horseshoe-shaped ring, up over the centre of the boulder – which is about the size of a small dacha – run his great-grandfather's violent indentations and marks. For the last number of weeks since, there's been a fire burning underneath, which will build the heat of the stone to a great temperature, they say, before they suddenly cool it with seawater and, they hope, crack it along its fault line. I imagine it will be fragmented and dispersed for the building of a wall or a house or a shed of some kind for the sheltering of animals or tools, but I do not ask. For the last two days, however, the fire has been raging all around it. Seeing such a thing in daylight reminds me of the furnaces in Kirov. Paulie Óg looks up and, noticing me approach, smiles. Then he gestures me urgently towards him. The wind picks up a knot or two as I jog over the strand, past the popping mud polders to where the smoking rock stands. I soon realize how loud this fire is. The smoke billows and blows and disappears and blooms again, wavering the air around it, as if this fire is somehow summoning the ur-nature of the rock back into being – reframing its stone-ness. Beneath and around the boulder are mounds of firewood, turf and gleaming coals. Great flames reach up, lick and fall. In three increasing rings around the stone are more belts of fuel, and it seems it is Paulie Óg's mission to add to these rings over the day. His hands are black and his face is already smudged with soot. His blue eyes seem like distant planets plunged into a receding dark. He steps from the fire again to let his eyes, which are now streaming, clear. He walks out along the strand again, then turns and walks back.

'You weren't at Mass,' he says, finally, throwing a handful of turf under the rump of the stone.

The heat from it is nearly unbearable to me. The fire hisses and cracks so loudly that I must raise my voice to be heard: 'I felt unwell!'

'Fr Dahjerti said nothing,' he replies, his hand shielding his eyes as he drops yet another shovel of coal to the fire underneath.

Closer to the stone, the heat yawns up. I stagger away.

'That's incredible,' I shout.

I look at the water gently lapping into shore not metres from this flaming object – the estuary tide has never seemed so uncanny.

'We need to get it up to a couple of hundred by night-fall,' he calls back, throwing some quartered lengths of ash onto the yellowing flames, 'then we'll give it a crack. Father brought a halved oil tank back from the mainland. We'll fill it down by the jetty, fit two staves across its underside and later tonight, when the stone's gone beyond hot, we'll carry the water over and tip the lot across it.'

I look over the unyielding surface of the rock.

'Wherever it cracks,' he shouts, 'I'll step up and hammer into the crevice a dozen of these wedges and I'll not stop beating the blasted thing until it breaks.'

I step away from the smoke, swinging with the breeze into my face, and I walk to the clump of metal wedges and crowbars, and the sledgehammer lying in the spare and sandy grass.

'I'll beat the thing till it splits in two. Mark my words, Nikolas!' he shouts.

I cannot tell if he is in one of his ironic moods, but the zeal in his work suggests that this young man is now utterly serious. It occurs to me that if he is successful – if he breaks this rock in two – he will suddenly find that there is nothing left on this island for him to do or see through, and he will be forced outwards and away, or, he will be forced to look inwards, and I am not wholly sure he is the sort of person who could sustain such looking for long.

I circle the rock again and survey its pocked and dimpled surface. It begins to suggest itself to me as a projection from a far more complex place than this.

'Be back here by nightfall!' calls Paulie Óg over the din.

I turn and make my way towards the purpling mudflats, the resting seashore and the harbour beyond.

In my gatehouse I light my fire and sit to read the newspaper once more. The roof timbers overhead creak in the wind, which soon subsides. I look over at the small and simple telescope standing beside the window in the corner. It points upwards, registering upon its glass the changes in light. Paulie Óg and I fashioned a solid if rudimentary tripod for it, and on clear evenings we would arrange it upon the strip of gravel between the rear of my gatehouse and my vegetable garden, and orient the scope towards a certain star or star-grouping. On clear evenings, when he did not visit, I would point it towards the moon and look on at the shadows being cast across its craters. I'd take a sheet from *The Times* and with charcoal from the fire draw onto the printed pages of tightly crammed text a crater. For an hour or two I'd observe shadows sliding across the surface of the moon. I'd section the double-page spread into eight squares and every fifteen minutes look up at the crater in question and indicate on the news-sheet the shape of the shadows being cast across the valleys and peaks of this part of the moon. From these altering shadows, I'd try to discern the form of the crater and its surrounding topography, and from this I would estimate how gradual or extreme the descent into this obsidian canyon might be, and from discerning so I could then, by looking over the eight incremental segments of drawings of shadow, guess at the manner with which the surface of the moon in that particular place had once been blown to pieces.

I go to this grid of drawings fixed to the wall adjacent to my fire; then I go to my small table, take out a sheet of writing paper and begin a letter to my sister. As I write, I realize that my heat towards her has become infected by our distance to each other. I realize too that my anger at her has replaced almost completely my hatred of her husband, Arkady – the source of this disdain. The last time I had contact with them was the morning after my brother's funeral, the morning after Arkady and I had exchanged words fuelled by vodka and mourning. I was always disappointed in my sister Varvara for being drawn to a Komsomol thug such as he. She is five years his junior and when they first met she had admired the strength of his convictions, convictions he made obvious ever since their days in the League of the Militant Godless; and before, I felt, she was old enough to know or judge better, she had already taken his hand in marriage. He was known by then to bully teachers in his technical school and the polytechnic he attended too, regularly having senior staff suspended by the Party. On the night of my brother's funeral I asked Arkady, he drunk, to desist from singing his petty Komsomol anthems. We were sitting in the small hotel lounge near my father's then home in eastern Kazan, remembering my fallen brother, Evgenii, in tones that were otherwise subdued. Arkady told me he'd not take orders from a pretend old-regimer like me. I could intuit he was playing on my association with Professor Rogkov and my time in Moscow and London. I told him that he and people like him, who hold their pencils like fence posts, ought to listen a little more often to men more suited to learning and administration.

'The likes of me?' he replied, slyly.

'Poorly transformed peasants,' I said, with a heat I instantly regretted, 'mere cadres making up his docile hordes!'

'Poorly transformed, you say, Nikolai Nikolayevich? Please explain.'

And to this my sister rose from her stool beside me and stood behind this Arkady Arkadyevich Peversev's chair, her hands placed upon his robust shoulders, and I realized he was not as drunk as I had first thought.

'You know,' he said, 'you don't insult me, Nikolai, as much as you do our leader and by extension your own family and your beautiful sister, whom I have grown to greatly admire.' Then, smiling broadly and while reaching back and patting my sister's hand, he continued, 'But you know that, don't you, Nikolai.'

By then I had stopped looking at this boor and had instead directed my gaze at my sister and I could feel my face harden with hers and my father's hands then harden upon my shoulders. He led me away from the glowing fireplace in the hitherto quiet hotel lounge, directing me towards its entrance, and home. As I left, I could hear behind me my brother-in-law breaking back into song.

Next morning, my father brought me a message from my sister and her husband saying that I should not come back to

Kazan again and that it was only on account of my being my sister's brother that I had not already been reported. It was a blessing I should make use of, my impotent old father insisted, in the kitchen of his small apartment, before he begged me to leave.

I write out my sister's name on the head of my sheet of paper, *Varvara*, and I try to dispel the hardness in her face, but I am unable to dissipate it, even in this phantom form. So instead I take to my bed and try to find some sleep in the growing darkness of the day.

Some hours later, when I wake on my stomach, my chest pulsing into my horsehair mattress, I imagine, in the dull part of my mind, my heart as a hammer beating downwards and enlarging a void, far below, where I feel I can at last either deposit my heart and unburden myself of existence, or from the echoes of this place, learn to accept myself. And in my waking breaths, and as I turn onto my back, I imagine from this point of acceptance a new windblown terrain opening out before me. I feel myself stepping out from behind a tripod and hesitating – unsure for a moment as to how I might take the measure of this new terrain.

I rise, go to the next room, lift a knife from the table beside the fireplace and score into the sandstone lintel above the window in my gatehouse:

Из этого окна смотрел Лобачевский.

Here once looked Lobachevsky.

3

I walk back up and over the hill to the school, the well, the houses, the harbour and this inferno around the erratic. Shouts and laughter drift up from the sea and empty themselves skyward. This was a clear end to the day and as I crest the hill, and where the hedges give way to the fields and the lower fields to the grey-blue mudflats and the mudflats to the sea below, the reddening estuary opens up to me again, as if it were for the first time.

While I descend I can see the houses now lie in the shadow thrown inland by the distant peninsula and in this dark it becomes apparent that all of the energy in this part of the island has been lifted from the huddle of houses, over past the harbour, along the shore, and has settled as it were around the giant flaming boulder. I can scarcely imagine what sort of heat is coming from it now. Such is the abandon in the cries, shouts and shreds of what sound like songs, I can tell some if not all of the men and women have visited the improvised still at the westerly beach and brought some of their pjutieen back up, and that they have begun to drink. Jim occasionally drinks whiskey too. He is the only one here who can bear it. On his birthday in mid-June last year, he and I, on the wall beside the well, drank a number of cups of whiskey, tipping measures of the well water into our cups. I don't usually take water in my whiskey, but I was curious to see how this water so heavy in lime would taste in whiskey – I found it agreeable, but still I couldn't quite understand why one would add any water to whiskey. I told Jim that I found myself most at home here whenever I am on a ganda-low in the estuary, floating between land masses. He nodded in what then seemed to be agreement.

Orbiting the glowing boulder cluster all four families, sitting intermingled on rocks, stumps and stools. Their faces flicker out from a dark that is otherwise now enveloping the place. As I stumble along the rocks leading to the shore, the sea waves to my right rush, fall and hush. The twinkling on the surface of the water can be seen at distances I cannot discern. It is what might be termed a still night. Most of the islanders are clutching receptacles of different kinds and are staring into the fire; some stand suddenly and step away from the heat and smoke, only straying as far as the light of the fire goes. Those that walk away seem almost bored and I intuit that they are here only in case they might miss something indescribable. Paulie Óg, hunched and covered over in glis-tening oilskins, is tending the fire. When he sits motionless he takes on the shape of a lesser rock. The fire below the rock glows, a ring of white heat being licked from moment to moment by the escaping vapour. Every now and then, after venturing too close, Paulie Óg steps to one side and his sister, Eta, throws a pot of water over his oilskins, producing great clouds and hisses of steam, only for him to return once more to the ring beneath the rock into which he throws further chunks of timber and peat and coal. The rising mist and smoke from his oilskins follow him in breaking drifts. From time to time the large red-headed Jim Guineáon replenishes the rings of fuel around the rock. He wobbles as he works, and I am sure he has already had too much to drink.

'Good man, Nikolas,' calls Guinan to me, 'you overcame your sickness. Come here and sit with us.'

There is an upturned bucket between Guinan and Jim Guineáon's wife, Rose.

'The fish was delicious,' I say to her as I sit.

'Very good,' she replies, gathering a swathe of her grey hair from off her shoulder. She takes a sip from her cup. I cannot tell if she is drinking whiskey or pjutieen or water.

'Would you go a drop?' asks Guinan.

'An amount of whiskey would be in order.'

'Good man.'

An hour later and Paulie Óg has told Jim Guineáon that he need not continue replenishing the rings of fuel, and that by the time the fuel they have is burnt off it will be near morning and 'the thing' will at last be ready for the water.

'We'll give it a crack then,' he says, rubbing his hands together.

The dark-eyed young of the Guinane family are led home to their parents by the four tired children of the family Guineáon. James takes a carbide lamp and they all file silently off – after its blue-white glow – for bed. Paulie Óg's sister, Eta, has fallen asleep, her head of curling black hair lolling upon Harry Geenaun's shoulder, her mouth open. Geenaun's daughter, blonde-haired Frances, sleeps at his feet. He sits staring into the fire. It flickers orange-and-brown light across him as his narrow eyes narrow further. If I were to bet, I would wager that he has at least at one or two moments this evening thought about his wife. He has a blue blanket over his knees and I don't believe he has moved much since I've arrived.

No one is talking or singing anymore. Just the hum and whistle of this inferno and the soft lap of the refracting estuary water. I want to tell them all that I will be leaving soon. I want to tell them all that I am not and have never been a Polish holy man. I am afraid, though, if I made such a revelation here that it might draw from Paulie Óg's focus, or worse that they might all laugh at the thought of them ever believing in the first place such a fiction.

'Will you come cutting with us Monday morning, a vijk?' asks Jim Guineáon from across the circle. He is sitting again now, with a white pewter beaker in his hands, an unruly tuft of his red hair massing like a horn from the top of his head.

'I will, Jim,' I say.

'Good man. We'll start early and get a nice boatload off to Kindara.'

'Very good,' I reply, though I know Jim often makes plans of this nature when he has been drinking and what transpires in actuality bears little resemblance to what was first proposed.

Rose, who has heard overtures of this kind from him many times before, is smiling cryptically as she gazes into the fire, her grey hair down once more across her shoulders. Her mouth hangs delicately agape, her tongue touching a chipped incisor, and she looks like she is on the edge of saying something, but instead she simply begins to laugh. She puts her fingers to her widening mouth. Then, she laughs out loud for almost five whole seconds. It is a high cascading trill. She tries once more to hide her laughter; then, as she becomes aware that she can no longer hide it, the less she seems to care and she merely leans forward and emits an abundant cackle.

'What?' says Jim Guineáon.

'Oh, Jim,' she says, stemming tears from both of her eyes. 'Oh, Jim, but you're an awful tool.'

And then not only she but everyone including Jim Guineáon begin to laugh. We laugh for a minute or so, one of those collective laughs that seems to increase in mirth out of a type of rhythm between laughs and guffaws and gasps and tears. Even Harry Geenaun is laughing and he has roused Frances at his feet and he has roused Paulie Óg's sister, Eta, on his shoulder too, and these two young girls are waking, in front of this blaze, into this world of joy. These girls do not laugh, though, they fall testily back to sleep once Harry's shoulders cease heaving and have returned to rest.

Everyone takes a sip from their cups. A waterbird cries from far off. Jim Guineáon produces and solemnly smokes a cigarette. Guinan's wife, Siuu, a sinewy, quiet and fair-haired woman, stands to straighten out her dress, then sits. Since I've arrived she has been studiously watching her son, Paulie Óg.

A great shuddering crack comes from the fire. We look to it, then to Paulie Óg, then back to it again.

'The last of the mainland ash,' claims Paulie Óg, who has pulled his scarf down from over his mouth and is drinking from a cup. His handsome face glows yellow. He passes the cup to his mother, pushes the scarf back up over his mouth, advances to the fire, stokes it with a snapped length of oar, then he stalks the object. He looks around it like a sculptor about to embark on a form hidden far within.

'What do you think, Pól a stjoorr,' says Siuu, looking almost plaintively at Paulie Óg striding about.

'I think we might be close.'

The sky has turned away from the black and somewhere behind us the sun is beginning to rise. The nights here during the summer are mere slivers of darkness. But now, still in spring, the load of the night is heavier. My face is hot from looking at the fire, but my back and the backs of my legs are cold. There is dew on the grass. I turn and take in the mist resting and shifting in layers of blue-grey around the top of the rolling navy hills on the mainland. Paulie Óg and Jim Guineáon leave in the direction of the harbour to join Rose, Guinan and his wife, Siuu, in hauling the halved tank of water back to pour upon the rock.

Harry Geenaun, who has rarely ever spoken to me outside of the business of work, asks if I have family. I tell him about my brother, Eugene, who died two months after the Siege of Leningrad – trampled by a retreating Panzer. I tell him about my sister, Barbara, who married a Bolshevik and has not spoken to me in nearly ten years. I tell him that Barbara looks like my mother who died giving birth to her. I tell him my brother and I once resembled our father, a coarse-featured and short-sighted man, who now lives alone in a small house on the edge of an expanse of bogland. I manage to tell Harry Geenaun all of this in a way that he could just as easily believe these phantoms haunt parts of Poland as they do Russia. He seems content to hear that I have also had loss in my life. He drinks from his cup.

Then, after some moments, he says, 'She was a lovely woman, Frances,' and he strokes his daughter's blonde hair. 'I met her at a dance.'

Guinan told me one day as we oared across to Motebeg that Harry, some months after Frances's death, had seen her crossing a field, heavily pregnant, as if she were going to the shore to relay an urgent message, but when this figure disappeared behind a length of hedge she reappeared as a grey hare that leapt away into the next field and fled. Guinan told me this in such an off-hand manner that I could find no reason to disbelieve him. That night, then, in my gatehouse, I imagined her delicate hare-form indentations dotted around this island – small voids dropping closer to any meaning the island might have, far closer to any meaning the names placed upon it might suggest, and I thought of those few months, in the early years of the war, while my snapped shinbone repaired itself in hospital in Leningrad. My bed was next to one belonging to a silent and emaciated Ukrainian soldier, found in a forest a mile from the front by a returning column of partisans. During my final month of convalescence, this Ukrainian began to eat and strengthen, and on occasion he would sit up and talk to me for a few drowsy minutes. His innards some days attacked him brutally and on good days left him in a sort of painless stasis. On one of these pain-free days, a few weeks before I was dispatched again, with weakened legs and body, to Kirov, to organize these frame-less paintings and priceless pieces of furniture, he told me about his journey back east. As he relayed his unbelievable hardships, I realized that he was the sort of person who had gouged his story into the surface of the earth, whereas I was the sort who had barely seemed to touch it. Then, one day in late March, the afternoon I was released from hospital, I met Matvei at a bridge adjacent to Moscow station. The city around us was a grim, smouldering ruin – as if someone had set a hand bomb off inside a horse's mouth. Matvei's face was colourless and hollowed out from his time on the front digging anti-tank trenches. He was bewildered, frantic at the thought of having to return west again to fight. We were leaning on the bridge parapet, smoke billowing disastrously from all over the city, and, as I told him I was being sent instead east to Kirov, a body appeared in the icy river water below us. It floated out from underneath the bridge, face down, bloated, but with the flesh on this figure's buttocks and thighs, long-stripped expertly to the bone. We stared at this half-corpse for some moments, then we looked at each other and promised that when all of this was over that we would meet again in Leningrad.

From the island harbour spring forth the raised voices of Paulie Óg, Jim Guineáon, Siuu and Guinan as they emerge back onto the beach. They are mere shivering outlines struggling with the halved oil tank – this heaving palanquin of seawater. The quartet stiffen under the sloshing weight, as Rose follows, looking on. Harry Geenaun rouses the two girls, and from behind a row of rocks he produces one then two then three small step ladders, which he opens in creaks around the stone.

The four figures carrying the water arrive, all of them covered in mid-winter oilskins, and with the sound of groaning timber and steel and the slapping of water they advance up and onto the rungs of the stepladders and pour with considerable grace the contents of the oil tank onto the smoking stone. The whole thing hisses, but within moments the hiss disappears into the crackle of the fire below. They retreat at speed back towards the line of light now enlarging above the horizon, leaving Rose, Eta, Harry Geenaun, his daughter and me to look on at this flaming and steaming rock.

They return from the jetty again, once, twice, three times and still the fire is not close to being extinguished. The older men and Siuu have their hands on their knees and are doubled over, straining for breath. Paulie Óg strides around the object, waiting and listening, his curls lank and drooping over his pale face.

'Not nearly cold enough,' he says, gasping, 'but we still have the chase of suddenness on it. Come!'

He grabs at one of the handles of the oil tank, but Jim Guineáon has toppled to the ground. He keels over mid-smile, mid-grimace. Harry Geenaun and I step to the oil tank and grasp a handle each. Slim and fair-haired Siuu, whom I feel would give her last breath if it meant helping her son succeed in his endeavour, takes another, and we proceed at speed towards the jetty once more where Paulie Óg and Siuu descend hip deep into the cold and oily water. We lift the brimming tank up onto our shoulders, grunt back up the jetty, then make our way together across the shore and back to the stone, which is now obscured almost completely in hissing steam and smoke. Paulie Óg, Siuu and Harry ascend the trembling steps as I back away and watch the gallons of saltwater cascade in uneven waves upon the stone, as if the stone itself is gulping in the water. They step down off these small ladders and wait, catching their breath again. We go once more. As we go, my arms begin to burn, my chest tightens, my legs shear in pain. We return, pour and go again. Then, we go again. Then we painfully traverse over and back once more. Then, Paulie Óg, soaked and groaning, falls back upon the scorched and sandy grass. His chest heaves dangerously for almost a full minute. He stands and indicates that he'd like a drink, to which his father, Guinan, fills then passes him a tin cup. Paulie Óg is breathing so heavily he struggles to find his mouth with the vessel. He takes two, then three shuddering mouthfuls. He spits the fluid out, shaking his head and wiping his lips with the back of his filthy hands.

'Water,' he gasps.

Jim Guineáon pours from a jerrycan into his pewter cup some water. He hands it to Paulie Óg, who is now bent down and staring at the blackened stone, which is surrounded in steam and great wobbling shrouds of wet smoke, and in the breaks of these clouds I can see the surface of the stone is being bathed in the red of the dawn sun. I look to Paulie Óg and I see how his creativity differs to Gusev's and how the violence of Paulie Óg's creativity then differs from Gunter Rhatigan's – Paulie Óg's is the violence of curiosity, and it is one he shows more readily than almost anything he says or does and the beauty of his type of violence lies in its unattached-ness to great or worthy causes. I hunker down beside him, and as I put my hand upon his shoulder, as if to offer my condolences, an almost imperceptible shunt passes across the upper peaks of the stone, as if the tectonics far beneath this small mountain have shifted. Paulie Óg pulls himself to his feet, but I have stopped looking at the stone. I stare now only at his exhausted face, and through the exhaustion comes the smallest change in tenor, as if he, in the moments since he has seen this tremor, this crack, has aged precisely one year. He smiles beatifically. Then he looks around and calls, 'Did ye all see that too?'

He grabs the jerrycan of drinking water and moves to the shore side of the stone, pours what is left in the can over the band of steaming ash at the base, as if he is hacking himself into a jungle clearing surrounded by great trees and vines of vapour. He steps into the gap in the smoke and puts his hand onto the rock. His mother, Siuu, shrieks as the flesh on his hand begins to sizzle, but he does not draw his hand away and we all fear that we may lose him – that there is a crevice in time so large in the stone that he might step into it forever. His father, Guinan, steps towards him and utters in a low voice, like how one might speak to a dying animal, 'Step away, a vijk. Please, step away to fuck.' Paulie Óg's hand has now all but disappeared into the rock and his face has changed from delight to a recognition of what he has done and his handsome young features darken as he pulls his hand from the stone. He turns from us all, holding his bubbling and blistering red hand in his other and he runs to the sea in almost total silence until he thrusts his hand into the surging knee-deep water whereupon emerges from his young and puckered mouth a whimper.

PART III

Square spins to circle. Square strikes circle. Both wobble, separate, counter-spin and in the background between them appears a bobbing pyramid.

1

I am standing alongside Gunter Rhatigan once more, at a level crossing on the edge of an expanse of bog. For the last number of days we've been touring the countryside in his new Morris Minor, and he has been presenting to me developments on the land. In the conversations between these updates on their technics, he told me about his fiancée, Una, and how Colm and Mel are both now in a district in the mid-West erecting electricity poles 'for the scheme'. Early today he and I visited a theodolite-stone on the peak of a hill forty miles south of here. In the mid-morning breeze Rhatigan fitted his theodolite onto the top of the stone and asked me to look through the lens. As I took in the rolling patchworks of distant fields, he said to me: 'That's miles of solidity, there now.'

A small locomotive trundles in from the east, drawing along behind it, in gentle clangs, an endless string of wagons heaped over with dark mounds of recently harvested peat.

To our right approaches a railcar, sending rags of exhaust into the air. It is unburdened. Rhatigan smokes a cigarette.

'Ancient empires vanish like morning mist,' I say to him.

'And they reappear,' he replies, 'with the clenching of a fist.'

He steps onto the railway, pulling a handkerchief from his pocket, and he waves it delicately in the air, signalling to the oncoming railcars.

We'll take that one out from here,' he says, gesturing to his right.

Twenty yards to our right the railway splits. One branch goes west to the power station in Gainston. The other is the route we are taking out farther into the bog, though I don't know where exactly it leads. A breeze rushes along the land, lifting eddies of dust and peat up out of the industrialized dunes and snaking eskers. I look around at the variations of brown daubed onto the lower reaches of a field of sky blue and white, interrupted in the far distance by the outline of a low hill, a chimney, a tree. As the train grinds to a halt beside us, a young man jumps from the cabin.

'That new curve you pulled, Gunter,' he says, 'the cant is much improved.'

He looks me up and down.

'Very good,' replies Rhatigan, 'yourself and Dan can take that load in. I'll take your engine out yonder.'

Rhatigan leads me towards this railcar and we clamber in. Despite the machine seeming quite new, the chamber already smells deeply of oil and peat and sweat. It returns me to Kirov on the first day I arrived there, my stomach low, worrying at the sudden mysterious displacement again from Leningrad. Rhatigan releases the brake. It clanks then hisses as he pushes on the accelerator. He holds the brake stick warily. I can tell he is new to operating such a machine. From under the window extends a yellow panel with circular dials showing speed and temperature and oil levels, and above these dials is fitted an ornate metal plate engraved with the words 'Hunslet of Leeds'. It must have frustrated them to go to England for this; they seemed to have done everything else around here without them. We lurch forward into what becomes a smooth acceleration. The scrubland passes then disappears behind a two- or three-mile-long finger of dark milled peat. A rhomboidal patch of evergreens slides past and then the land opens out into a raked and smoothened desert of brown, with this wobbly railway line extending in front, bisecting the ground. The sun's rays streak across the windscreen.

'I want to show you what kindly development looks like, Nikolai,' he says.

I look to him and he can tell that I don't quite understand.

'The developments in your country, Nikolai,' he says, eyeing me, 'stemmed from a hatred of the Czars. Our projects emerge from the wish to show fairness to our fellow worker, not hatred towards what came before.'

I say nothing.

'Do you get my meaning?' he says, from the side of his mouth.

'Yes.'

'And do you agree?'

'It would be possible to convince me.'

The railcar groans up an incline. Rhatigan pushes the accelerator forward and we ride the rise. As we trundle down the other side, the land opens again but now with gatherings of short and tall buildings emerging in the distance. Rhatigan brings the railcar to a halt and jumps out.

'Follow me!' he calls, as he stomps into a seeming wasteland of bog.

I leap from the car and follow. Even this unused land feels far drier than when I was here before. Rhatigan walks on another hundred yards, then stops and turns, and pointing to the ground says, smiling, 'Do you recognize that old thing?'

Three feet proud of the peat still hovers that steel disc with its face of fading red-and-white circles.

'Damned thing,' he laughs. 'I asked them not to move it.'

He points to the mid-distance, and I can see a number of stubby stakes leaning in the ground.

'Are the nails still in them?' I ask.

'Oh, we fucking cursed you that week,' he says, and, peering around, continues flippantly, 'but we got on with it.' Then, looking back down at the circle above the peat, he says, 'Don't you lot love your relics. Take a good look now, touch it, then move on from the front of the queue and let the others cop a feel!'

I look to him, and then in the distance over his shoulder I spy the twinkling power station sending handsome spirals of smoke into the air.

'I was glad when I heard he was dead,' I say.

'I would say you were not alone,' he replies.

The wind rises, funnels, then is sucked across the land towards invisible fleeting origin points. Rhatigan moves off, and for a moment I close my eyes to see if I can still feel the ground below move. I feel only the merest of tremors.

We return to the railcar and Rhatigan, keen to deliver us in among the buildings in the distance, puts the engine into a higher speed. As we inch along, I look out over the land to the left and see five men of varying ages handworking a tufted row of sliced-up bog. Beyond them, a Turf Board toolshed is being constructed; a crane on caterpillar wheels lifts pale roof-truss triangles into place. I look back at the bending and straightening labourers, and their slim wooden tools cast at angles alongside their carefully built stacks of criss-crossing turf.

A cigarette each, and half an hour later we shudder into the centre of this complex of buildings. To the right sprawls a construction site of mostly low-rise housing. We walk towards the front edge and to the most-complete of the buildings, where we traverse further planks and jump some puddles, walk past men shovelling aggregate into a clattering cement mixer and enter the frame of a house of concrete-block and timber.

'The bog-manager's sitting room,' says Rhatigan, smiling. 'I'll be in here with Una by next Easter.'

I enter the next room and can see through a window-opening more of these houses stretching away in urban-like rows – a tiny Saint Petersburg, a freeman's Kalinin. The farthest and largest building has a crucifix cast into its structure.

We ascend a ladder to the first floor and enter a meagrely proportioned rear-facing room.

'Space for a toilet and a bath,' says Rhatigan, still smiling.

I imagine him, in less than a year's time, pulling himself naked from the bath in here, drying himself vigorously, putting on his bedclothes, turning on and off electric lights, and entering one of these rooms and climbing into bed with his new bride.

'The bog-manager's abode,' I say.

'I'd to lobby the minister for the baths,' he replies. 'They said it was a luxury too far, putting in facilities. So I asked him, if, after a day's work whether the workers would feel revitalized after a wash and then I asked the minister if this fine feeling might not help all of these thousands of workers sleep better and work better too.'

Rhatigan's natural fervour has altered since I last saw him. He seems more Soviet than me.

'You will have many fine nights of sleep,' I say.

He leads me to a front-facing window. A breeze passes in over the bog, making the room feel incredibly cold. Sunlight chased by shadows passes over the land until it falls dull once more.

'All this would have been much further on had we not to heat the Dubs during the war,' he says, then he points to three large cylindrical buildings placed in a stagger across the land opposite.

'Experimental station, briquette factory and labs.'

'You took good note of Kirov, comrade!' I say, to which we share a staid chuckle.

As we walk around the incomplete briquette factory all I can hear is the wind rattling the corrugated roofing overhead and the clangs and grunts of men erecting a metal frame. Shafts of light break into the dark through the gaps in the asbestos sheets. Rhatigan tells me about the 'peco process' they hope to employ here, how they will squeeze the last of the moisture out of the peat before they mix it once more and bake their briquettes. He often indicates to empty spaces, asking me to visualize a process I saw many times before in Kirov, over a decade ago. He has become, as the actualities of his plans have neared his dreams, a bore.

'Is this what you wanted to show me?' I ask.

He retracts his hand mid-sentence and looks somewhat burnt. I realize I have asked my question too curtly. It dawns on him that I perhaps do not care much anymore for such things.

'Just infrastructural developments is all, Nik. Don't worry, I'll not keep you. There's an archaeological finding further out that I'd like you to see, though. They found a thousand-year-old body there some weeks back, then a section of road and such. It's holding us up, but it might be of interest.'

Rhatigan walks us with a cool thoroughness through the other two buildings, explaining their workings and ends, almost as if now he is rehearsing a script for a visiting dignitary. He tells me they hope to have this complex finished by next year; he tells me they are planning to host an international symposium on peat and that they have begun work on a publication called *Peat Abstract*, which they hope to soon make available to other nations invested in this kind of extraction.

'We hope to become world leaders,' he says looking upward to a narrowing shaft of light.

I walk towards him and embrace him. I take him in my arms and I tell him that I am proud of him. I tell him that it is men like him that make countries like these, and I tell him that this beautiful country deserves men like him. I unhand him. He steps away. He looks, for a moment, as if he might strike me, but instead he fishes his cigarettes from his pocket and offers me one. I take it.

'That island got into your bones I'd say,' he says, lighting up. 'It has you a-wanting.'

'Maybe,' I say.

He laughs insincerely. Then leans to me with the flame.

As we walk back out into the daylight, I tell him about my quandary with Malenkov. I tell him an old colleague in Leningrad has written back to me saying she can't take the temperature of Moscow for me and that perhaps it is too soon to return. I tell Rhatigan that Beria has released millions of non-politicals and that Zhukov has been returned from his banishment in the Urals.

'I even wrote Malenkov a letter to his Granovsky Street residence,' I say, as we climb back into the railcar.

'And did he reply?'

'A mere standard state missive, acknowledging receipt.'

'To the island out west?'

'Yes, a few weeks before I departed. They will now most probably know my new name too,' I say.

'I see.'

Rhatigan releases the brake. We roll beyond the three cylindrical buildings and the complex of unfinished housing, and rejoin another expanse of industrialized bogland. To the right lie rows of milled peat with enormous harvesters travelling up and back, and to the right of this, towards where we had come from, another machine raises great chunks of this ancient material, splits it and pushes it to one side – where a line of railway recedes – and these split chunks of peat are then dropped into a waiting wagon and rolled away.

The weather, as we continue into the bog, alters from dry, fine and warm, to dark. The clouds gather over us with alarming speed. It's the sort of change I've seen rush over the flat expanses of land here many times before, but have somehow forgotten the shivering thrill it gives me. It seems more unexpected here than the swift changes in weather I became accustomed to on the island. Soon it is raining. Giant drops explode onto the roof of the railcar. Rhatigan turns on the windscreen wiper. It scrapes grimly at the glass. I open the door to my right and thrust my hand out into the rain as we go.

While raindrops plop onto my palm I sense Rhatigan shift awkwardly beside me. He continues to shift in this uncomfortable way until he eventually ventures, 'The football matches, Nikolai, you know, they sound much different now ...'

I look to him as he continues, pensively, 'With all of the new folk, I mean – the bogtrotters in from the west and down from the north. We used all just mix together, fans from other local parishes and what have you, and you couldn't tell who was shouting for whom,' he says, pushing a strand of white hair from his brow, 'and I used to like shutting my eyes at games and enjoying the difficulty in distinguishing who from whom.'

I picture Rhatigan standing on an incline beside a pitch, he in among scores of flat-capped men, smoking and laughing, his eyes shut for some moments trying to intuit the sounds around him. Then, he continues, telling me with what sounds like sadness how these relocated workers now gather together in cliques into sections of the stands and shout in unison to their teams, 'as if they know the words to the song,' he says, 'and,' he concludes, 'that this singing has ruined what once was diffuse in the sounds at these games.'

I peer over to Rhatigan and I can see that he is troubled. I imagine behind his newfound confidence still lie acres of doubt. Looking at this Gunter Rhatigan I can see the guilt that first drew me to him and that drove his sense of industry has now been pushed too far inside the core of his churning drive and this guilt that I wanted to view once more, so as to perhaps learn something more about it, now certainly lies embalmed, utterly detached and forgotten.

As the clouds course and gather in the sky and the rain begins to fall again, Rhatigan seems to relax and almost take pleasure in the shelter given to him by this metal box rattling over this segment of industrialized land. He turns off the wiper and waits for the windscreen to fill with raindrops to the point that one, should one be attempting to peer out of the windscreen, would not be able to see with any clarity what is approaching, should anything be approaching. He continues like this for almost two whole minutes, then he turns on the wipers again and this pushes the water to one side, then the other. I creak open my door and take a rag to the side window to wipe it clear. In the rear-view window appears in the distance what looks like a man on a motorbike, chasing after us. I show this to Rhatigan.

'The part! I forgot that bloody part!'

A minute later and the rain has drifted away. We are walking alongside a line of empty parked-up wagons towards this distant buzzing motorcyclist. The strip of land to the side of this railway is rough and wet and at times there are large gaps in the ground. It is a poor carriageway for motorcycling on. The man skids to a halt before us. His young face, goggles and all of his work clothes are covered in specks of blackened peat. He hands Rhatigan a bulging leather sack.

'For Dr Vajril,' he says, before turning and zooming away.

Over the next hour and more Rhatigan tells me about the first rows of mechanical turf he saw being cut and turned and loaded here. I can discern his pride recollecting in him as he describes the progress. He tells me that though the hand has been taken out of the bog, it still hovers overhead managing the technics that traverse it. Then he tells me more about his fiancée, Una. He tells me she is the eldest daughter of one of the older bog-worker couples that have moved here. He describes her to me in a way that at once acknowledges her beauty and charm while also making clear that he considers her to have married upward. As he speaks it occurs to me that he has become convinced in the intervening years of the idea that, in this new country, a man of action can become a man of power and a man of power can become a fringe of an establishment; and it seems to me this new organ of technically adept, bureaucratic and secularly religious men see no hypocrisy in forming so easily this new establishment in a country that seems to have only recently, and with great difficulty, rid itself of a long-standing and hostile power. It becomes clear to me, as Rhatigan speaks fondly of his new wife-to-be, that what fuels this new establishment is self-fulfilling myths of being at once among and above those that deserve.

I tell him about a beautiful country estate an hour outside of Leningrad, which had the most well-managed gardens, grounds and stables in the whole of Czarist Russia, and I tell Rhatigan that this house, which is now a mere curiosity on an Intourist route, was once the site of the most callous of murders, where the Czar, his wife and his children were all shot one after another, before each other's eyes, each knowing that the last to live, the youngest, would live longest, however briefly, with most burden. As I recount this story to Rhatigan, who remains unmoved, the quiet dark-eyed Guinane family come, for a moment, to my mind, they solemnly bending and cutting and throwing wet seaweed onto the blue mudflats sweeping out the width of their segment of foreshore, and I imagine the fear the last of the Czar's children must have felt when the Bolshevik gunman trained his gun on this child's head, and this thought indicates to me the other side of the fear that must pervade the house of Guinane, and I suppose, as I fall silent – while looking to Rhatigan, standing beside me in this rattling railcar traversing this empty bog – that the intensity of waiting felt by the last person of a decimated family, however briefly, must make for only a distant shadow of the fear that inhabits the whole of a family waiting for the loss of the first. And I realize, before I begin to speak once more to Rhatigan and to break the somewhat awkward silence that has grown between us, that though these two feelings might be projectable across some firmament – one folding imprecisely towards the other, and back – they are still only projections made up of the very driest lines of connection, and not even sight-lines, and certainly not lines from any source of light. They are lines I would do well to rid finally from my thoughts and my person too.

As the light towards the west begins to lessen, a row of fluttering tents – large, small, cuboidal and peaked – rise into view.

'Dr Vajril's commune,' says Rhatigan, 'the archaeologists. There's a row of hoppers full of peat beyond; but let's first tarry here a while.'

We trundle up to the group of tents, disembark and step towards the centre of this gathering, where the rail line comes to an abrupt end at the edge of a large oblong-shaped pit, with ten or perhaps a dozen people walking around within.

'Here's where we found the first segment of bog road,' says Rhatigan, 'and then, underneath, they found the bog man. Such luck!'

Dr Vajril, a tall upright individual with high cheekbones and thinning blond hair approaches. If someone were to tell me he was Norwegian I would not have disbelieved them.

'A special visitor,' says Rhatigan to Vajril. 'Nikolai Lobachevsky is here with us today.'

'The Russian geometer!' exclaims this Vajril. 'Ah yes, the men in the power station told me about you, and your lightning conductors!'

He is smiling.

'And you fled west then, I hear.'

I avert my gaze from this Vajril and wonder how many people here know about my movements.

He laughs and pats my back as the wind picks up. It blows his thatch of blond to one side. He flattens it back down with the palm of his hand.

'But you're back with us now, good man.'

He directs us past the first hole and on to the edge of another larger but square-shaped pit and therein stand motionless another number of young people all of whom I guess to be Vajril's students or apprentices. It looks, for a moment, like a still from a film telling the story of a great tragedy. Then, one of the characters moves and the whole scene clicks then whirrs into life – the young people begin to step, heads down, searching.

I can tell we are at another sort of crossroads, but one that criss-crosses time more than space. Extending either side of this pit, at almost a metre below the surface of the bog, runs what looks like another railway, but one made of dark lengths of ancient timber.

One of the students below straightens. She pushes, with the back of her muddied hand, her dark curly hair from her handsome young face and she indicates to Dr Vajril that he should return to the pit and inspect what it is she has just found.

'That's the bog road,' says Rhatigan, gesturing with his chin at the corduroy of gnarled planks either side of the pit.

Dr Vajril, steps into the base of the pit, then hunkers and begins to brush carefully at the ground. He rises, takes his camera, dangling from his neck, and carefully composes a photograph.

'Christ, they've found something else,' says Rhatigan, 'that'll be another week of this tipping and tapping.'

I leave Rhatigan as he seethes at these curious people nosing around in his mulch, and I step around the pit. Dr Vajril moves away from the young student, climbs the pit ladder and he approaches me as Rhatigan appears to my left.

'We have photographs of the bog body,' he says, smiling. 'Would you like to see?'

I nod and Dr Vajril strides to the largest of the tents, a brown pyramid of canvas, its flanks billowing then flapping in the wind. Some moments later he reemerges as Rhatigan noisily clears his throat and spits. Dr Vajril produces three photographs: one of the pit showing the location of this body, then one of the maroon-coloured figure being lifted and loaded onto the flat bed of a railway wagon, and the last showing this leathery body up close. Dr Vajril pauses at the third photograph, his finger hovering over the image. We look at this torso and half-covered skull, arms up either side, and I realize that this is the position my brother, Evgenii, slept in as a child, face down with his fists up either side of his head – or at least it is in this position he would be when I would rouse to him in the morning.

'I curse these turf developers as much as I love them,' says Dr Vajril, grinning.

Rhatigan shifts his weight and lights a cigarette.

'This chap died making his way through a copse of willow, we reckon,' says Dr Vajril. 'He was attacked from behind, with an axe, or sacrificed, there's no way of telling exactly yet, but he was a large and robust lad, most probably a leader on his way to some ritual in some place of importance.' And he looks to me and licks his lips.

'And how did ye get on out beyond?' asks Rhatigan.

Dr Vajril gazes to the left and gestures vaguely, 'We're pretty sure now that the road runs out to what was once an island – little more.'

Rhatigan pivots away in a show of lack-of-interest as Vajril turns his vague gesture into a sweeping one, and continues unperturbed, 'All of this would have been wooded in willow, hazel and birch and perhaps even some alder, you know … Imagine this land filled with those handsome waving trees. And our guess is that from the island there's another road back to the drier land extending into that purlieu between sod and soil,' he says, pointing towards the sun in the west, its lower rim meeting the horizon, '… but again, we can't know for sure until we get all of this back to Dublin for testing.'

'A land bridge over a swamp?' I ask.

Rhatigan looks at Vajril, but Vajril is frowning back down at the young ancient king in the photograph.

'No,' he says, now squinting into the breeze, 'more likely a land bridge into the bog, but again …'

The young woman with dark curly hair, who has been digging and brushing with a controlled excitement for the last many minutes, straightens once more. She calls up to this Dr Vajril, 'I think you're right. It is a wheel!'

He bounds from us, and steps back down into the pit.

Rhatigan peers over at the railcar and its line of peat-wagons sitting ready.

'You'll have seen more Irish bog than most Midlanders, Nikolai,' he says.

I can tell he wants to leave. He calls down to this Dr Vajril, telling him he has the part for him, and he drops the leather sack in a clump of heather at his feet. The dozen or so young people stepping carefully around the base of the pit have now gathered around Dr Vajril. He is talking and gesturing to them about this new find. He forms a circular shape in front of his chest with his fingers, and I wonder what it is he is imparting to them. As his students close in around him they reveal the rest of these remains, all dotted with tiny white flags, squares of string and red-and-white lengths of timber denoting points and places of importance.

As Rhatigan and I depart, stumbling over the peat towards the railcar at the prow of the trail of hoppers, he tells me that long before that corpse was a living man this whole area was once wetlands and then for a few hundred years when the temperatures rose the land dried a fraction and in rushed acres of trees and it was from several hundreds of these enormous oaks and ashes, all reaching up out of the systems of hummocks and hollows, that the planks for the old bog road were sourced. 'Or so Vajril tells me,' he concludes, as the scent of bog water passes in from somewhere far off to the south.

We climb into the railcar. It is a similar model to the one we have left behind, but it seems to smell more sharply of human sweat. Rhatigan fires the engine and slots the mechanism into gear, and the machine sends shudders up through our legs and bodies. It groans then whines into life and progresses for some minutes, building momentum as we proceed out into the plains, covered over in purpling heather at first, then thinning and opening again out into well-worked and bare terrain. Behind us the wagons bump and clank in a way that might be described as macabre.

'You should bring French out to this dig,' I say.

'I should,' Rhatigan replies, 'but he passed on there last Christmas – found collapsed between his house and his sheds.'

'Oh,' I say.

I picture the mud in his yard. Then I imagine his pristine objects lying inert in his huts with light slowly edging across them.

'You know I visited his museum.'

'He was telling me, one of the days after you left. He said it was a shame that you only saw a fraction of it. He said it was a shame you ran out of steam.' Then, as the railcar rattles on over a bump, he concludes, shaking his head, 'Never mind. Doesn't matter.'

The landscape around us begins to alter once again. The sun has almost completely set, drawing what was once red in the light away and leaving in it what is mostly blue. The surrounding terrain seems to have become more orderly. An empty church with a pointed roof in the style of a Soviet train station veers into view, and beside it the beginnings of a giant glasshouse. In the distance between the two sits another squat cylindrical building, but with a slender onion-looking dome to its top.

Again Rhatigan follows my gaze. 'We'll make insulating boards for the walls of the houses in there. All from turf gasogenes,' he says.

The air becomes cooler as we pass, and the land becomes darker. We rumble alongside well-planted rectilinear woods, then rectangular fields of wheat, and I note the sudden and total absence of hedgerows. As the wheat fields in the distance pass, I notice long cobbled roads between, and consider this stretch of industrialized land as a decent environment for people to carry out their work. Rhatigan by now has fallen completely silent. I cannot tell if he is troubled, or, if he is troubled, what it is that troubles him.

'Do you ever think of him?' I ask.

To which Rhatigan says nothing, and all I can hear is the engine and the oily clang of the rail passing below.

I look at him and the land sliding past outside, and I gently ask once more, 'Your brother, Gunter; do you ever think of him?'

Rhatigan, with a firm grace, reaches across the railcar and takes hold of my throat. He eases me up against the window. I stumble, flail and try to say his name, but I can suddenly no longer breathe and I cease to feel my feet. I attempt to gasp as he pins me there, he still looking straight ahead at the oncoming land. Then his fingers begin to close around my neck and the vibrations from the railcar rattle into my skull. I swing my arms at him, scratching his cheek, but he simply pins me there, my body at once squirming and weakening. As my chest and throat begin to thud, he turns his gaze on me, but his eyes have emptied and I can see what is drab in his industry and that the companionship I'd hoped from him has become now irrelevant, below even a companionship-in-theory, and what I was hoping to learn from him about forgiveness and guilt he will not be yielding, and, yet, I still cannot breathe, my temples bloat and the railcar itself has begun to darken, and entering into the outermost edges of this terrifying dark appear tiny stars. My spine and legs buzz as I flail once more at Rhatigan's adamant outstretched arm. He merely pushes my neck back farther until my Adam's apple distorts my windpipe into a curve around my spine and now there is absolutely no air coming in or out, and I can hear someone, perhaps me, far away, gasp for anything like air. Rhatigan pins me there, his mouth downturned, my body now shuddering under this crystallizing arrangement of pain; then, his pupils are drawn left. His eyes widen, and his hand drops from my neck. He puts it to his mouth as if, in the distance behind us, he has seen something more awful. My body, climbing out of the encroaching dark, burns, to the point that I do not want my body anymore. I collapse. I stagger to my feet, then bend over, heave and cough as the railcar bumps over the land. Then, looking on as these fleeting stars fall away as the shadows that held them return to the daylight, I peer up at Rhatigan and I can make out that his gaze has now altered into disbelief at what it is he sees in the distance.

I turn, gulping and touching at my neck as my windpipe opens, in folds, and I look out of the window. In the distance I see a machine of such size that it seems to be felling fifty-foot stands of evergreen, in swathes, like how one might scythe down wheat. Giant thuds and thrums shudder from this distant machine. I look to Rhatigan, but he is now frowning as much as staring. He rubs his eyes and looks closer. His hand trembles over the brake and I can tell he is unsure as to if he should stop and investigate this strange machine. I can tell also that he has put what occurred between us already from his mind, and I realize that this void in him has an engulfing indifference from which I want to remove myself as soon as it is possible, before it begins to expand and raze what has meaning to me: a belief that what connects me to my past is worth keeping alive. The railcar moans as we approach a slight but long incline in the bog, and Rhatigan knows that if he halts the locomotive here he will lose the momentum needed to overcome this incline and we will be stranded here together for the night. So we proceed up and over the climb, and progress farther into this endless-seeming bog where to the right, as if suddenly pushed up from the ground, emerge scores upon scores of giant five-lanterned streetlamps edged in ceramic sheaves of corn, the lights atop all flickering into life. Rhatigan, now mute, stares on, but still we continue, until alongside the railcar appear a string of workers in a purposeful march. They consist of old women and young men and they are trailed by a string of dark and underfed whelps, trotting in a line. I look away, then in horror look back and realize the headscarves these old and stooped country women are wearing have the hallmarks and patterning of the headscarves belonging to the women I used to see from my railcar near the power station at Kirov. I turn to Rhatigan and, in a painful rasp I scarcely recognize as my voice, I demand to know where he has brought me, to which he replies, looking now almost pleadingly at me, 'Nikolai, I am sure we are on the right road, only because there is no other!'

I push the window down and croak into the closing darkness some Russian words to these old women and young men. I ask them why they are here and what they are doing. I ask if they are workers for the Irish Turf Board, to which they stop and simply applaud us gently on our way, as if we are a column from a returning army parading down a broad boulevard aimed towards the east. One woman, dressed in red and green, breaks from the ranks and approaches our railcar. Though hunched, she seems to be a large person – of well over two metres – and she brandishes what looks to be a bouquet of local flowers: asphodel, rosemary, sundew and myrtle interspersed with dots of bog cotton. She has gathered the whole of what is romantic of the bog into a fist of shivering colour. She follows us till we traverse the next rising, whereupon Rhatigan pulls the brake and we grind to an echoing halt that triggers a rising notation of clangs from the wagons behind. We disembark and this large Roman-nosed woman approaches slowly up the embankment, she bowing, slightly out of breath, until she presents Rhatigan with these flowers. He takes them wordlessly. She tells me that she was born on the bog and it is on the bog she will burn. She speaks in heavily accented English and I ask her from where she procured her headscarf. She tells me they are a collective, these women and young men, and they make these headscarves and cravats for each other. Then she and the large gathering of women and men far behind her begin again the most gentle performance of clapping and bowing. I realize it is a performance shot through with a delicate irony of the kind I thought only existed in my homeland. The women and men descend the rail embankment, depart and continue – with their half-dozen or so whelps in tow – their purposeful jog back across this land to the far edge of which rests a sliver of a faint and disappearing sun.

As Rhatigan and I roll across the dark of what remains of these wide lamp-lined terrains, I realize that what is reemerging into the pit of my stomach is the bile of home-sickness. It is as if some great obstacle has suddenly been removed from my gut and into it flows again, at last, the loneliness of not being near those who speak and move in ways I made patterns from as a child. And, I realize, I am no longer willing to trade my beliefs for what it is I am denying myself, and I resolve to go to my sister, Varvara, and beg her for forgiveness, if only to glimpse my mother again, or at least what is hosted of my mother in my sister's face.

PART IV

Shadow cast by pyramid travels over the lower vertex of triangle; circle spins past in the background, followed in the distance by an oscillating square.

1

I feel like I have seen this place before. I'm facing north into the deep grey of a morning mist and looking on at the distant shadows of cargo boats. They chug over and back across the English Channel between long-agreed points on one coast and long-agreed points on another. It is cold, even for a morning in mid-November.

A middle-aged woman in a tweed dress-suit and hat appears, stepping down along the gangway. She stops a few metres from me, nods and she then too turns to the sea. She takes from her leather handbag a cigarette and a petrol-fuelled cigarette lighter, one of those Lumets I saw advertised a few years ago, when I first I left the mainland and went west. I pull from my coat pocket a crumpled cigarette and I ask this woman for a light. She smiles and leans towards me, thumbing her lighter into life. The flame flutters in the breeze. I turn back to the deck railing and we smoke in silence. A boat passes. Then, shivering, she elegantly casts her cigarette overboard, nods to me once more and walks back along the deck to return indoors. I rub my face, place my cigarette between my lips, thrust me hands into my pockets and close my eyes to the wind.

I spent the night in the eastern side of London with this old college friend, Smith. We last met when he visited me in a damp cellar-apartment near Hyde Park, while I was waiting and moving and waiting, over the course of those winter months, for my Polish passport and my return to Dublin. Yesterday evening he treated me to a meal, with two friends of his, both young promising writers. Before they arrived I told Smith about my aim to return home and to seek forgiveness from my sister. He looked sidelong at me for some moments as if to suggest that he did not think my plans were wise. Then, he simply embraced me, saying, 'Life has become better, comrade. Life has become more joyous!'

He'd gone to great lengths with this meal. The table, though small, was crowded with food and drink: bowls of potato salad, a plate of liver paste, beetroot, radishes, bread, lettuce, herring, glasses of vodka, wine, lemon tea. We ate and we drank and we talked and smoked until almost three in the morning. I left his townhouse quietly at six for my dawn train over the Norfolk floodplains to Harwich, then, with my drink-headache beginning to bloom, I boarded this boat. When I am tired out by alcohol in this way, I prefer to be in the cold rather than in warmth, and the fusty warmth of the seating section inside this creaking boat is so busy and full of people, that to be alone on this frigid deck is, for this moment, smoking and now looking on at the silent boats drifting by in the distance, perfect.

One of the young writers I met last night, a tall man called Rolley, referred to Stalin as having been little more than an 'unimpeded pig farmer', and that what he has left behind throughout the Soviet Union is little more than a series of sties. He used the word 'slatternly' more often than once to describe my country. I could tell by comments of this kind, coming from an Englishman of a lowly if artistic position, that his beliefs, like marrow through bone, stem from a conviction that without a land-grabbing navy, no matter how powerful or enormous a country is, in the eyes of men like he, this powerful or enormous country will never truly be considered an empire. I told them about the bogs in Ireland. And these young writers, both of them city men, sat up when I described to them how the water table in the place affects the nouns one might use when looking upon this land. I told them that the meaning of the word ascribed to a patch of land in such areas as these as much bubbles up from below as is designated from above; but whatever the name given to this land, it can only be used from a distance. You would not name the land as you walk across it, I said, in case you might somehow destroy it and then drop into the void of what it is you have poorly named. I told them about the man's name 'Tiurljok' and how it refers also to small lakes in limestone regions that come and go. I told them that in October of each year these bodies of water appear most often as mere ponds ringed with yellow flowers, and in the summer as soft domains of black-green land often covered over in grazing animals.

The deck on this boat has become now too cold for me to stand here any longer. I put my cigarette out, pull the collar of my woollen jacket up and stamp my feet a while, then return indoors to the benches, the rustling newspapers and the few tired and crying infants. I take my seat on the wooden bench once more, opposite a young mother and her boy.

The boy, who is dark-haired, can be no more than five years of age. He wordlessly climbs over his mother every couple of minutes until she rights him beside her again. I can tell, in her patience and the lack of heat in each repeated righting of her handsome boy, that the child is simple. He makes for me, arms spread, but his approach is suddenly halted. He stares, groans and I realize that his mother has fitted him with a harness, not unlike a leather bridle, but one fitted snugly across the torso. The halted, staring, healthy boy is wrenched back onto his seat. He continues looking at me until I can look at him no more. I look to his mother, but she is peering at her son, reading him for a moment. She returns to her book, while curling her son's leash in her fist.

I peer out the window at the inexpressive skies. Then I pull from my pocket a letter from my cousin Ivan. I wrote to him during my last few days in the Midlands, telling him I was travelling to Kazan to see my sister, and he told me I was welcome back from the wilderness and that I should come and bide with him as I returned east through Berlin.

I look to the letter, it merely saying: 'Dear cousin; please come forthwith!' It occurs to me as I look to the address at the head of this inexpensive paper that he must by now be living in this Pankow district of the city for almost half of a decade. I imagine him as settled. I have not seen Ivan for many years and I realize that I'm looking forward to seeing him again. His mother and my mother were close sisters and this closeness Ivan and I happily mimicked on the occasions of family visits when we were very young.

I look back to the boy. He is snoozing. His mother, whose hair is thinning around the crown, reads on and seems content. We are still hours from the Hook of Holland.

2

As the train pulls away from Hannover station for Berlin I find myself sharing a bench with a young man with a black dog. The dog is old and each time the young man rises to put on a coat or to take his flask or food box from the luggage stored above, the dog lifts its head to ensure this young man is not straying far. I sit and doze fitfully, waking only as the train passes the snow-covered landscape outside. I dream of my brother. It is the first time I have dreamt of him since I left the island. My dream is of him as a young boy lying in a bed beside me, sleeping, and in the dream I can hear my mother at the end of the room, beside a fire, humming an old traditional Kazani folk tune, while above her shadows from our bedside candles and her fireside candles flicker out fleeting geometric shapes upon the ceiling.

In Berlin I walk towards the Pankow district in the north-east of the city. My belongings, such as they are, lie folded in a timber-and-canvas suitcase Paulie Óg and I fashioned a few days before I left the island. That night he gifted me one of his comic books too; it lies now rolled up within a shoe. We made the suitcase in my gatehouse, in near silence.

Earlier that day I'd seen a partial eclipse of the sun. I'd directed my telescope skyward and where the sunlight passing through the scope struck the floor I placed my notebook and watched the bright circle on the page become encroached upon by another darker one. The birds outside fell silent. Even the wind that had been bellowing around that bright day fell quiet too. In the eclipse-gloaming of my by then near-bare gatehouse, I realized that the sexual exile I've placed myself in since Matvei's death had taken the form of a chamber, which had altered in aspect around me so completely since I'd entered that I'd forgotten where the entrance to this chamber lay, and I wondered, if I ever did find that entrance, would I choose to leave or not. Then, the tiny circle of light on the ground reappeared, only to be burned off by itself as the light outside and inside my gatehouse returned to the lovely midday luminescence of before. That evening I returned to Paulie Óg the telescope and gifted him my newspaper-drawings of the craters on the moon. Some nights later, on my last evening there – as we shared some fried fish and some plums – he asked if I felt I was living life well. I told him I knew no better way to live it.

Later that night, before I took to bed, I looked at the bare rough stones of the house wall where my drawings had once gently hung and occasionally in a breeze crinkled and billowed, and it occurred to me looking at the shadows on these stones flickering in the light of my one lamp, that the mesolithic monuments made on the earth a long time ago must have been as much measuring tools as they were objects of reverence to celestial light-giving bodies. I considered it then plausible that a mesolithic human, while constructing a monument that might take generations to build, had used the six-monthly intervals from solstice to solstice as a means for measuring against the sun the layout and accuracy of the monument being built in reverence to it – I came to realize standing before that wall that the mesolithic ring of stone, or the burial chamber, or crux was just as likely to be an object that used the sun to orient itself across the land and into the shape of its supposed reverence as it was an object made solely in reverence, and I wondered why our belief in these things as only objects of reverence seems to have pushed away what would have been pragmatic in these mesolithic people and the building-use they would have derived from the shadow of the sun at dawn, on a day that it can be trusted, casting the shadow of a corner of a portal stone onto a useful point on the ground.

It is bitterly cold now walking through these broad and wan Berlin streets. The snow and sleet, through the darkness between the buildings and the doorframe-filled ruins around me, is sweeping about in murmurations of dull then sparkling white.

By the time I arrive at Ivan's apartment there is a stove lit, a samovar issuing sweet-scented steam and some food prepared for me to eat. He embraces me warmly. Then, moving to turn down the flame in his samovar, he tells me that I unfortunately cannot stay long, but that he would be honoured if I took his bed for the night.

Before we sit to eat, I go to the next room to write a letter to the mother of my friend, Matvei. I recalled, as I was travelling across the German countryside to Berlin, that I had once promised her that I would return his papers to her, papers that were handed to me on that evening in the train station office in Leningrad. These papers still lie in my desk drawer in my room in my apartment.

I say in my letter to Matvei's mother, Yelena, that I will visit her upon my return to Russia and I will at last bring Matvei's papers with me too. I tell her that I would like to spend a day and a night with her in Oshra and to exchange stories about Matvei, and tell her what he meant, and what he might have meant, to me had we been able to spend more time together. As I linger over this letter to his mother, I remember, in among his papers, that he once had scribbled extensive notes about a scene from a film he must have wanted to make. The notes contain a length of script and some directions on camera angles and movements and certain playful innovations in shooting he felt appropriate or merely just exciting. The scene involved a man and a young woman talking to each other, the man on a train-station platform, the woman standing, 'in a plane of light', at the door of the train, looking through the lowered window. They are in the early stages of love and the woman is unsure. She does not want the man to come with her. I transcribed their conversation into my own notebook. At quiet times and after long intervals I sometimes read these notes and often try to visualize what it was Matvei once tried to imagine. I open my notebook out to read again these cramped notes I made from his. The writing is so small I can barely see it in this lamplight.

Woman:
(To the man on the platform, smoke issuing from the engine in the distance.)
Help me be a strong-jawed June.
I told you before – I promised mother that I would never allow you into my life.

Man:
Just for that I'll not see you again.

Man storms off.
Woman retreats from the window.
Camera cuts to interior.
She looks sad, alone.
Camera passes over this woman's shoulder and floats down the centre of the train, then, it pans left and is directed out the carriage windows, following this man stomping off on the platform below.

Camera cuts to an exterior shot of the man walking.

The man has second thoughts, stops and turns back
towards the carriage door.

Cut to the camera in the carriage as it floats (reverses)
back up through the centre of the train until it arrives
back at the woman at the door, still looking upset.

Camera cuts back to the simple external shot.

The train begins to pull away from the platform.

The man breaks into a run.

Camera cuts to interior.

The woman's face brightens when she hears him call
and his footsteps approach the door.

Camera cuts to woman's POV.

(What she sees is in colour – these frames will be coloured!)
We see a close-up of his hand grasping desperately onto
the window.

She places her hand on his.

He pulls himself up and appears at the window, the
wind blowing his hat from his head.

The train station in the background slides by.

Camera cuts to exterior (the camera fitted to the train
and angled upward at the man).

Everything is returned now to black-and-white once more.

Camera now pans up to a view of the passing heavens
filling with smoke.

Man:

I was thinking, suppose I asked you to marry me?

Camera cuts to interior corridor framing woman and man.
The woman looks away, then looks back.
Camera cuts to close-up — framing only the woman's
face in the centre of the shot.
She is smiling widely.

Woman:
Kiss me goodbye. And we'll travel together next time.

And to this promise, the man's head appears from the left of the frame and he and the woman kiss tenderly. 'This will be a new way of looking, of showing!' thought Matvei — and in his notes at the end of his pages of scribbles and drawings and glyphs, he claimed that the dialogue in this scene could itself be a kind of summation of his innovation, an innovation, I realize, that disintegrates colour and space and the divide between traditional framing devices ... and this, I could intuit from these scattered notes, dreams and crossings-out, was something Matvei in his final moments had hoped for — to deliver something new in his art through an act of devotion in it.

I finish my short letter to Yelena. Then I stand, address the envelope for her home in Oshra and I leave the letter on the small bedside table for posting. I go to the water closet a few floors down and pass a painfully bloody stool. I strike a match and see the blood on the bowl is clotted and dark. My illness must surely have spread inwards, though I am yet to feel it there. I return to the apartment, and Ivan, who is now merry with drink, tells me about this Block 40 on Stalinallee that they are helping to build and the uprising he and his colleagues took part in during the summer. His three friends who have newly arrived are also glassy-eyed. They were seeing off, at the train station I had just come from, three friends returning east to work on Rudnev's Palace of Culture and Science. Ivan's merry housemates are handsome men, and they are smiling at me too. Their smiles are pained, though. They sit and begin a game of Terzo with faded pink cards that look to have been made from the cuttings of the pages of an old instruction manual for a machine of great size. Ivan pulls from a cupboard over the stove a sack and tells me in his coarse country Russian about the packages they've been living off since July.

'Peas, lard, flour, pasteurized milk ... *Yankee dreck*,' he says, and laughs, 'but it is enough. And the funny thing is, Nikolai Nikolayevich,' he continues, with something of a slur, 'I don't mind putting up our buildings in this city. I am happy to stay here and to help us hold our ground!'

Then he breaks out laughing again, and I can see in the dim light of the kitchen that he has lost a number of his front teeth. He and his friends, then, lowering their voices in a more lurid than covert way, proceed to tell me that in a cellar nearby they still have a store of unexploded mines, which they bury in craters, or ruins around the city, or where they know the local 'rubble women' will begin their clearing and stacking work again. These men tell me they enjoy the idea that their 'gifts' will be found long after they are dead. When I fail to find much humour in this, they straighten from their crouches, harden, and the kitchen falls into a slowly imploding quiet, punctuated only by spits from the fire. Ivan, who I have not seen in over fifteen years, I realize, has thickened over the shoulders, and has become insincere. When he was a young and shy farmhand visiting us in Kazan, he was humble, and when his humour broke through his shyness it gave off light; now it gives off only darkness or perhaps his humour is something that sucks upon light. I wonder were these three shorn-headed ex-soldier friends of his also once young and shy boys. I am passed a glass of vodka, from which I take a sip; then, I take another. I sit and smoke a cigarette with them. I ask Ivan if he has heard from my father or my sister, to which he replies with an emphatic: No. Then I leave for bed, to sleep without eating. They implore me to return, as if I am about to miss an evening of memorable conversation, but I shake my head and leave.

Ivan's bed stinks and the room is meagre and draughty. I remove my spectacles, and as I lie on this bed scratching at my anus and my neck, the wind now howling outside, I can hear the men next door laugh and croon. I had forgotten I'm exhausted and that I still have a long trip ahead of me to Warsaw tomorrow.

Before I sleep I think about Paulie Óg and the last time I saw him, waving to me from the island on the cold and misty morning I departed. As he disappeared from sight I realized he was the sort of person, if left long enough alone, that might develop the curiosity to drop himself into the unspeakable lands below the category of 'human' and while there he might see or even sniff around at what is unfathomable and aterrestrial in the individual, while pushing back with all his will against the enacting of such categories as: woman, man, human, Irish, Russian … and in doing so he strikes me as the kind who might uncover what is truly alien in himself, and others, such as me.

3

I wake to the outline of a man in my room. Another joins him, then one more. Then one carrying a lamp steps in and gives them form. They advance and I am pulled from bed. I grasp for my spectacles as a sack is thrust over my head. I cry out for Ivan. My arms are wrenched around behind my back. I struggle and then I am stilled. The sack smells of hessian, blood and many other men's mouths. I throw up into the sack. Then I retch. I hear Ivan's voice, 'Wait a moment! Please!'

I can smell his breath and feel his hot forehead against mine. As he whispers, with great urgency, all I can see in my mind's eye is a mouth and teeth: 'Forgive me, Nikolai. And when you see my dear mother, ask her to forgive me too. They are taking you to Hohenschönhauser.'

The men behind have wrenched me past him, but Ivan has taken hold of my arm and he is shouting to the men, 'Please, one last thing! You owe me!'

I am held by the shoulders, and I can feel my shoes and my foot clothes being removed and all I can hear is Ivan whispering below, at my feet, 'Forgive me, cousin Nikolai, please, forgive me.'

I kick out at him once, then twice. But one of my feet is already bare. I kick out with my shodden foot once more.

I wake on my stomach. The back of my skull aches. I roll and thump around on wooden planks and from the sound of the engine and the passing carriageway below I can tell I am in a delivery van of some kind speeding somewhere through the city. The sack is now revolting. There is glass tinkling around within it – a piece of lens. I would give anything for this sack to be taken off my head, for even one moment. The van accelerates up a hill and I slide and roll backwards then it takes a corner on a syncline and I skid and roll once more. On it goes, this jerky painful trip and I imagine these men are not actually travelling far so much as dumbly circling a district of the city in the hope of disorientating me. Round and around they speed.

The truck comes to a halt and I hear the front carriage doors swing open and closed, and as the doors open behind me, a chill breeze blows in, meeting the undersides of my feet. As I am dragged across the planks of this truck, a splinter enters my thigh. I land on my stomach. I lose my breath; I can feel wet snow. They untie my ankles from my hands. I am kicked in the face, then raised, gasping to my feet. My jaw feels dislodged. My molars, when I grind, do not meet. I can feel the wet snow on my feet change to cold then dry concrete as I am led indoors, down some steps, across, then down further sets of spiralling stairs, then more, until I am led into another corridor, then down another set of steps and into a space that feels hot and smells of men. The sack is taken from my head and I am pushed into a pitch-black room. I fall onto the ground and am greeted with a snicker. There are four or perhaps five men already lying on a wooden bench. The place smells of urine, wind and bodies. I step in something soft. I fumble for my spectacles.

'First night you sleep on the ground.'

I sit on the edge of the bench and put my glasses on. I am struck by six different fists across my head and shoulders.

'The rats,' one of them says. 'One night with the rats.'

The door opens and another man is pushed into the room.

He is drunk and collapses on the bench. He is shoved from the bench and falls in the rectangle of space beside the bed, where I myself was about to lie. He is ossified. I bend and remove his shoes and his foot clothes and I put them onto my feet. The shoes are too big but they are warm. I stand. I lean and slump.

After an hour and more I hear a voice from the darkness below.

'Your name?'

I answer.

'Crime?' he asks, and I can see a dim glinting rectangle in the shadows and I discern that this man has at least one gold tooth.

'I do not know.'

'Well; you won't be here long.'

'How long is long?'

'I've been here a day. This snoring thug beside me, two. He is here the longest, our senior cellmate!' to which he laughs.

'Yours?' I say. 'Your crime?'

'Oh. Like you. Do you have any strings that you can pull?'

'I do not know. Maybe.'

'Well, I would say that you should pull them now.'

And this man, whom I cannot see, falls back to sleep. A line segment of light appears under the door. I realize that for the first time in many years I cannot guess what time of day it is. There is blood still oozing from my thigh. The splinter is lodged in my muscle. Each time part of this muscle tautens the rest gathers into painful spasms that shoot up and down my leg, towards my knee bone and up to my hip. I pull the ragged shard of timber from my leg and as I feel the skin rip around it, out pops more blood. I can feel it flow then trickle down my leg. I push the wound closed with my knuckles, and I think back for a sore moment to the colourful ribbons and rope I once erected in Leevee's hotel bar, and I wonder what is being muttered and what is not being muttered in there now, and is the sun coming in the front-facing windows, or is it late at night and is the place at rest and is Nell ghosting another room upstairs, presenting her body and her breasts to another unsure man.

One of the cellmates stirs, tumbles over two of his bedfellows, kneels at the edge of the bench, and in his half-sleep relieves himself into the bucket at the head of the man passed out below. A creature scuttles across the floor, maybe two. I consider the pain this passed-out and drunken man will feel tomorrow.

A set of footsteps pass. I shout and rattle the door, 'Please, may I speak with someone. There has been a mistake. I have made a mistake!'

It is greeted with a thump.

The footsteps round a corner and the line of light at the base of the door disappears. I lean back into the corner of the wall and consider weeping, but it is too dark, too filthy and I am too thirsty to weep. My trouser leg has stuck to my wound, and the material has congealed into a knot around it.

4

I wake to two men leaning over me. They are in uniform
and they wrench me by my arms from the ground. I come
to as I rise. I picture a child-like grimace on my face. One
of these men looks to have himself only roused recently.
His face is pale – his blood must be low in iron. The shoes
I was wearing have been removed and my fellow inmates
are standing to a strange attention along the wall beside the
bench. They are of comically varying heights, gazing like
soldier-marionettes ahead at the opposite wall not two yards
away. I can see in this weak light that the walls of the cell
have been smeared in what looks like blood and faeces. I am
shoved alongside these men. Three names are called and the
three men to my left respond in turn. Sacks are put over their
heads and they are taken. The door closes behind them. The
two men to my right, breathing heavily, lie down onto the
bench. I imagine their faces wincing.

Some minutes later from far above I hear three gunshots. The cell quakes. I sit down on the edge of the bench to steady myself and look into the dark. I think about the letter I have written to Matvei's mother, sitting on the table in Ivan's room, and I hope that Ivan will destroy it and that he will not, out of some misguided feeling of guilt, post it to her, and have her then think me a person who frivolously makes then breaks a promise.

After some time the door opens again. We are forced to stand alongside each other once more. A name is called and the man to my left responds, 'Yes.' A sack is put over his head and he is taken squirming and screaming from the cell. The remaining man, stinking of drink, lies down on the bench, groaning in pain. Again, many minutes later – I think, but I cannot be certain; time surely differs in the dark – the sound of a blow from above is followed by another shudder through the walls of this place. I lie onto the bench beside this groaning man.

I realize that I may not have much time left here, so I decide to think about my mother, but I cannot see her anymore – the algebra of her face will not set; her bones will not come together here. Instead a bright afternoon in my gatehouse with Paulie Óg comes to my mind. We are standing over my white enamel basin and I've placed a hair from my head onto the surface of the inside curve of this basin. I then pluck another hair from my head, lick it and place it onto the outer curve of the basin, at right angles to the hair on the inside face, and I say to Paulie Óg that though these two lines in one sense intersect, that in another they will never meet – to which he nods silently, his handsome face pursed in concentration. Then I pluck one more hair from my head, lick it and place it flat onto the table beside the basin. Then, turning to Paulie Óg, I reach up to the crown of his head and gently pluck a curling strand of his hair. He smiles as I leave this half-spiral of hair down an inch to the right of mine. The delicate curve shines in the daylight breaking in the window of my gatehouse and I tell Paulie Óg that what interests me is a world where these four hairs are projections of each other, casting themselves, over and back, into seemingly different forms while retaining what is valid in their essence. He nods, indicating to me that he in some way understands, or at least that he will remember.

The door in the cell wall cracks open again and two men enter. The groaning man and I stand once more.

One of the voices behind me asks, 'Enemy Lobachevsky?'

To which I reply: 'I.'

A sack goes over my head. The sudden return to blackness makes me yell and twist until I am struck in the back. I feel a vertebrae crack and something small has come loose somewhere. The pain spasms in labyrinths down my spine to my pelvis and uncouples control from my legs. I twist, turn and wrench once more until I am struck again, and in this pain I relent and realize that what is holding me are hands far larger than those belonging to the two men behind.

My wrists are bound together as I am frogmarched up a corridor and many flights of stairs, and all I can smell is the hessian, and the blood and many men's mouths, but different men from the time before, and either this is a different sack or many men have been made to use it since. I am half-carried, half-directed down another corridor, up many flights of spiralling stairs and out into the open air. It is cold. The sack is old and I can see now, in the loosening squares of the weave, daylight. The slim layer of snow on the cobbles gives way to ice, then water and stone. My feet slip. I stumble, but I am caught from behind before I fall. I hear sea waves coming ashore. I am led into a shade and told to stop. The hands that held my arms fall away.

A man, behind me, puts the end of something to the back of my head. It feels like a circle, but one warmer than the air around it. He is not laughing. He says that he has a message for me from Leader Malenkov.

A cuckoo, from somewhere beyond the walls of this place, calls.

'Yes,' I say, as the metal circle taps the back of my head.

'Leader Malenkov told us that when you are caught that we should lead you to the realm of good people,' says this man, whom I can discern from his voice is young, is from the far eastern regions of Russia, and that he cannot and does not understand the considerable humour in this message.

I stand and wait, but can think of no reply. A dog barks from somewhere behind me. I clench and open and clench a fist.

I ask can they remove the sack.

The man whose voice I have discerned as being young must have reached forward and pulled the sack from my head. I see a crack in my lefthand lens, and beyond it a wall of brown pockmarked brick fills my field of vision. I can feel a hand on my shoulder and I can tell from the lightness of his touch that I am shaking. I can hear this young man utter to me a gentle, 'Shhhhhhh.'

'Thank you,' I say, as the metal circle meets the back of my head once more. It seems to bounce there a moment; hover. I close my eyes and await a trajectory I will find hard to compute and harder still to understand. I can smell that rain is coming and I can guess that when it falls it will quite likely melt what is left here of the snow. I would like to picture my mother one last time, but I realize this is not the time for that. I hear the tiny clink of metal meeting metal from somewhere far off to my left.

I turn my head, hoping to see a fellow geometer or a stone-splitter of some kind beating another mark into the ground, but instead I see only a distant moon being swallowed by a lifting tide.

References

A Moriarty Reader, edited by Brendan O'Donoghue, The Lilliput Press, 2013.

Education and Social Mobility in the Soviet Union, 1921–1934, Sheila Fitzpatrick, Oxford University Press, 1979.

Four Sides Full, Vona Groarke, The Gallery Press, 2016.

Gulag, Anne Applebaum, Penguin Books, 2004.

Man of No Property, C.S. Andrews, The Lilliput Press, 2001.

Measuring America, Andro Linklater, Plume, 2003.

On Stalin's Team, Sheila Fitzpatrick, Princeton University Press, 2015.

Rambles through Kilcommock (volumes 2, 3, 4), Paddy Egan, self-published, 2005–11.

Ten Thousand Saints, Hubert Butler, The Lilliput Press, 2011.

The Gothic Enterprise, Robert A. Scott, University of California Press, 2005.

The Place Where I Was Born, Paddy Egan, self-published, 2019.

Turing's Cathedral, George Dyson, Penguin Books, 2013.

Werckmeister Harmonies (2000), director Béla Tarr and Ágnes Hranitzky.

How to Proceed (2018), zoo – Thomas Hauert (dance performance at Centre Pompidou).

Acknowledgments

My thanks to Niamh Dunphy, Ruth Hallinan, Anna Benn, Peter Straus, Colm Tóibín, Hannah Westland, Luke Brown, Dr Maurice Casey, Viktoriya Kalashnikova, Feargal Ward, Paddy Egan, Marianne Gunn O'Connor and Nora Hickey M'Schili. My thanks also to Michele, Sean, Emily and to all at Askeaton Contemporary Arts. Thanks also to Anne Horrigan.

Thank you to the Arts Council of Ireland from whom I received a visual-artist bursary while writing this novel. So too to Literature Ireland and Centre Culturel Irlandais, Paris, who made possible a residency for me in late 2020, which enabled the completion of this work.

Thank you to The Lilliput Press and especially Antony Farrell, who continues to encourage my efforts.

Finally, my thanks to Seán Farrell, who edited this book.